of

Shattered

Cressen Books LLC
Gerrardstown

Copyright © 2013 by Rachel Stark

Cover design by Rachel Stark and Danielle Gesford
Cover Photography by Danielle Gesford
Cover Model – Caitlyn See

All rights reserved. No part of this book may be reproduced in any form or by any electronic or mechanical means including information storage and retrieval systems, without permission in writing from the author. The only exception is by a reviewer, who may quote short excerpts in a review.

Cressen Books LLC
Gerrardstown, WV

Visit our website at www.cressenbooks.com

The characters and events portrayed in this book are fictitious. Any similarity to real persons, living or dead, is coincidental and not intended by the author.

ISBN-978-0-9831013-4-5

Library of Congress Control Number: 2012956542

Printed in the United States of America

Contents

Dedication v

Acknowledgments vii

Lost 1

Shadows 11

Leon 35

Plans 50

Anchored 65

Treasure 82

Scrabble 103

Trapped 123

Shattered 131

Memories 150

Epilogue 173

Dedication

For Kenneth Preston Kimble
&
Johanna Maxwell Kreyenbuhl

I know you would be proud of the person I have become and I wish you could have been here so I could share the joy of publishing my first novel with you. What I have inherited from you lives on, inspiring me and strengthening me.
I keep you in my heart always.
All my love.

Colossians 3:17

Acknowledgments

Special thanks for this novel go out to Ed and Wendy Lohr for their patience, guidance, support, and keeping me well fed as a starving college student. Without you guys this novel would not exist. To Beasley's Books and Eccentricities for nourishing my creativity with the coziness of your café and yummy sandwiches. To my sister Emily, who let me wake her up in the middle of the night to listen to my stories and ideas over the years. And to my parents, friends, family, and teachers for all your love and encouragement over the years, always believing that I would be an author one day.

Huge hugs and a very special heartfelt thank you to Danielle Gesford and Caity See for this gorgeous cover. You both have been so amazing and I cannot express how grateful I am to have two wonderful, talented friends like you.

"All that we see or seem is but a dream within a dream."

~ Edgar Allan Poe ~

Lost

"Well, the name's Randy and ... I uh... well... and I think this is pretty much bullshit…"

…Where am I? And who are these people? My vision is hazy, but through the fog I notice the room we are in is large and wide, filled with light and chairs. I look around, the person speaking (Randy was it?) is sitting a few seats over from me with his large faded-tattoo arms crossed over his chest, looking disgruntled. The man he is talking to, a kind-seeming person with thick-rimmed black glasses and dark hair pulled back in a ponytail, listens intently.

"Randy," the man with the glasses scolds lightly.

"Seriously Doc, the only reason I'm here is because my probation officer made me." Randy's eyes shift around the room to everyone else.

Beside him sits a young girl whose features are blurred to me, and beside her, directly across from me, is a woman so light and pale, that I blink my eyes to make sure she isn't a ghost or just a trick of the light. There are others, like a young gentleman sitting on my other side who is staring interestedly down at his feet, and a guy and girl pair right next to him who are more one person than two. Their twin gazes are attentive and wide, soaking in Randy's every word.

"I've been clean for two months now, and I don't need to sit around and discuss my "feelings" with a bunch of lunatics."

"Randy, come on now. This is a safe space. Remember our rules, privacy and respect. No one is judging you."

I reach my arms out in front of me and examine them and then reach up and touch my face, my hair. *What is this place?* I glance over at Randy, listening closely for any clues. I feel the hard back of the chair push my posture upright and I cross one of my legs over my knee. Randy gives the ponytailed man an indignant look, and the man noticing the hint, quickly changes his approach.

"Perhaps maybe you'd like to talk about something else instead? What about your family?" the ponytailed man encourages. "Do you have any children?" Even though I was not remotely part of the conversation, the question seemed a little invasive. *Why should I care if Randy has a family or not? I don't even know who Randy is!* I shake my head to myself and luckily the gesture goes unnoticed. Randy actually looks surprisingly sentimental at these questions. He uncrosses his thick arms and runs one of his large hands through his scruffy dirty blonde hair.

"Divorced," Randy grunts, replying quicker than I had expected, perhaps quicker than anyone expected. A few people from around the room give Randy knowing stares. Except for the ghostly pale woman that looks familiar; she is staring at him almost with… envy?

"Divorce can be very difficult," the ponytailed man asserts. Randy seems like he wants to reply but pauses, waiting for his questioner to continue. When the ponytailed man remains silent, Randy adds, the words flowing out of him, "She found out I was on the H. The hard stuff. I was out of control. We both knew it. But she couldn't handle it. I wanted kids, you know. " Randy admits uneasily, his eyes glazing over suddenly, and I wonder what memory has stolen him away.

My heart pangs for him and the pain intensifies and settles in my chest, filling the cavity with some unknown, distant, but overwhelming sorrow. The intensity pierces sharply, acute to my senses, and I begin to wonder where I am again. I focus on the pain instead, following its path, trying to locate its origin. It is not Randy's pain, but my own. I am barely aware that Randy has stopped speaking.

"Thank you for sharing that with us, Randy. That was very brave of you," the ponytailed man says and then turns to the girl sitting next to Randy. A young woman, or child rather. She appears young, perhaps younger than me, maybe not even in her teens.

"Good to see you again, Emily. Do you have anything to share with us?" he prompts gently. She begins speaking, but my mind carries me a million miles away, like a veil has fallen over the present, muffling her sounds, her face, her aura. Shielding me. Covering up something that I want to forget.

Though I cannot make out her words, the girl is speaking rapidly and I feel my heart rate increase to match her tempo. I think I knew a little girl once, maybe. The inclination is strong, but an invisible hand is gripping me, pulling me farther away, and tugging on the pang in my heart. I don't resist and wait patiently on the other side of the veil. And when it parts, the spotlight falls upon the face of the figure I recognize immediately, the pale, ghostlike woman seated across from me.

A woman, early thirties, so pale that she was glowing ethereally, like the sun was shining through her, frail and wispy in the extreme as if she might just fade away at any moment. She makes me uneasy and the sorrow creeps up on me, channeling itself through her. Her familiarity only makes me feel worse; it makes me engrossed with her. I want to talk, to say her name, but it will not come to my mind.

"Charlotte," the man with glasses addresses, "Why don't you tell us a little bit about yourself as well?"

My breath catches and I am almost craning to hear her. If anyone can tell me where I am or reveal anything at all, it will be this woman. Her eyes are bulging, looking like they might explode with all the content in her weak form. And like a dam breaking, her story gushes out of her ashen lips, shuddering as each word leaves her mouth. I shift my hands, I do not want to hear her, but I do all the same time. Her eyes lock onto mine, looking at me with a desperate stare that I cannot break.

"He was the love of my life," she begins slowly and the raspiness in her voice is unsettling, "and I would have done anything to make him happy. I never saw myself as anything to love. But then he came along. He made me feel wanted, useful, like I was somebody." The woman takes a deep breath, "That's all I had ever really wanted." Her words now come tearfully, and her breaths more ragged, "But then there were some things that I couldn't get right. Any normal person would have, and I just needed to be told, but I just know that I could never do anything right. But I stayed with him, even when I wore out his patience to the extreme, it was always my fault. After everything he had done for me, taken me in, given me a home, I failed him time and time again." She continues, tears now streaming down her face, "and I t-tr-tried so hard to be better, so he would l-l-love me."

"I cleaned and cleaned and cleaned, but it was never clean enough." The ghost woman expresses mournfully and then falters, sucking in an uneven breath, "It was never enough. I could never get it clean enough for him."

"So I went to the only other person that I knew, his mother, and I said, you have to help me win him back! My desperation was her triumph and she used it against me, influencing him, blaming me, blackmailing me so she could manipulate him." She gasps on a ragged sob and lets another cascade of tears fall. The whole room is immersed in her tale. The man with the glasses doesn't interrupt; he looks at her, kind eyes wide, drinking in her story. "My heart was broken from that day on and I knew I was a complete failure. I had turned on him in the worst way. And with all that filth in my heart, I had to find a way to purge it."

"The first sip burned. It tore like fire through my throat, washing my insides raw. But I welcomed the fire, and time after time again, I let the fire consume me, and the drink take me under, punishing myself for all the wrong I had done, forever thinking that I deserved nothing."

The pain and sorrow in my own heart is pulsating again, branching out and throbbing, almost to the point of incapacitation. The throbbing pounds in my head, trying to pull me away. In the back of my mind, I see the ghost woman cleaning; she is scrubbing until her hands are raw and bleeding. Blood mixes with the soap and water. She curses herself over and over again, tears now mixing with the rest. Her tears become the burning river of white-hot liquor through her veins, numbing the derision of her fantasy.

A flash of my own memory is burning in me now. I try to push back a budding fear and the overwhelming sadness that has now found its origin, but the ghost woman's words release the floodgate. Screaming, a desperate sound full of terror, seizes me and floods my ears; bright flashing lights blind me. The whole room goes white but the screaming doesn't stop. And I realize that it is me.

"Katerina, sit down!" The man with glasses interjects forcefully.

But my screaming doesn't stop and the bright flashing lights replay over and over in my head, mixing with the blazing river of the ghost woman's torment and my own. My eyes yank open wide and search the room frantically for an escape. Breathing rapidly, my heart rate accelerates and I feel as though my lungs might explode inside my chest. I cannot be here anymore. I can't be in this place where the pain is trapping me.

"Calm down Katerina, take it easy now." The man approaches me, but his calming tones can no longer reach me. He starts toward me again and I am backed up against the wall, trapped. The room fills with a panic. People are staring fretfully up at me from their chairs.

"S-S-Stay away from me!" I yell and try to make a mad dash past him. I'm shaking because the fire is real and my whole body is set aflame and a river of tears starts washing down my face, but it cannot put out the fire. I stand against the wall trying to gulp in mouthful after mouthful of fresh air, but I feel like I am drowning. I look to the door and a group of men and women all dressed in white are moving quickly toward me. They grab ahold of me and I squirm under their firm grasps, but they keep pulling me under the water.

"Sedate her, now!" one of the men orders and I realize he is the one who has me in a vice-like hold. As the air slips from my lungs, I manage to utter one last scream as I watch the sharp thin end of a syringe plunge directly into the side of my thigh. The room whirls around and I am swaying and then falling…falling…

Shadows

"Kitty... Kitty!"

I awake with a start. Allie's voice rouses me from my sleep. The remnants of the dream are still dancing in front of my opened eyes. I rub my thigh; the pain of the needle had felt so real and it still lingers. *What was happening to me?* I bolt upright, rubbing my eyes as the shards of my dream lay fragmented about me. Staring through them into the darkness of my room, I try to remember the dream. Something about people and a man with black glasses, or was it black hair? Anything that is left over evaporates quickly and is gone.

Allie is here. I hear her picking. Picking like she always has with her nubby little fingers at the peeling nickel coating on my bedframe. I feel the pressure of her leaning in towards me and hear the creak of the mattress springs from her weight.

Allie should not be here. It is the same thought that I have every night. For a second, I strain my ears into the blackness, listening for the softest sounds, the antecedents of heavy thundering footsteps. But there are none. It would have been too late to hide anyway, too late to do anything but wait and let the paralysis grip you until morning.

"What?" I try not to be irritated.

"Kitty," she says my name in a whimper. She is afraid. Kitty, she says, not Katerina. Katerina is for the daytime. As in, *you're not my mother Katerina, so stop trying to tell me what to do.* She's only five, and sometimes I feel like she could be older than me.

"What?"

"I'm afraid."

"I know."

I grope into the darkness, knowing she is close without having to open my eyes. I can sense her small body trembling only a few inches away. She senses me too. Our hands meet, old friends teaming up once again for their midnight ritual. We pull each other into an embrace. Allie is here. I feel her warm breath on my skin and the curves of my body fill up with her tiny shape. I pull the covers over us to ward off the night.

"Kitty."

"What Allie?"

"Are you mad at me?"

"No Allie."

"I had a bad dream."

"Me too," I admit. "But it's okay now."

And everything is okay. The dead air is now replaced with the hum of two breaths and two hearts settling in. I hear her mumble in the dark.

"Kitty."

"What Allie?"

"Are you worried about tomorrow?"

"If we just follow the plan, everything is going to be fine. You'll be catching your dumb crawdads by noon."

"And?" Allie asks, her tone rising. I feel her rise up on her elbow. She is looking at me, expectantly. I can't see her face in the darkness, but I know.

"And, I will be reading my book." I answer.

Allie sighs. But I ignore her. She sighs again, a huffing, exaggerated sigh that tells me she won't go to sleep unless I finish our phrase.

"And, I will be reading my book, in the hammock, between the two tallest pine trees." I finish, slightly exasperated.

"Good-night Kitty."

"Good-night Allie."

We lay in quiet for a while. I open my eyes and look up at the ceiling. Even in the dark, I know that there are exactly thirty-seven wood beams above us in this room. I close my eyes so lightly, imagining them, counting each slender slat, one by one.

From my light doze, my body is jarred awake suddenly. I don't know how long I had been asleep. I glance toward the tiny window above the bed. It is almost dawn. From the thin rivers of barely-there blue light glimmering onto the floorboards, morning has almost come again. It is a false calm, a false beauty. A heart would wrench at its fleeting life.

I rouse Allie from her slumber, but she doesn't wake suddenly. The soft cloak of the night still cuddles her, guarding against a morning that each day I dare not to come. She rustles in the sheets, sprawling her tiny legs out over the covers. Being everything that is good, she gives me a reason to fight even though I have no desire to do so. Allie has no idea how much she looks like our mother, so soft and light with her beautiful long chestnut hair flowing around her face. Where the world is held together by mixtures of concrete and steel, working together to make the other stronger and more durable, she is gold, soft and malleable, but so very precious.

"Hurry now Allie, it's time." I whisper with urgency, but not enough to make her worry.

She stirs slightly once more, but the room is growing lighter by the second. Slowly she raises her arms straight out in front her chest, wanting me to hold her.

"Allison," I groan and lean down to hoist her small body up onto mine. Her eyes are closed, but she is smiling.

The sun is almost up. I have waited too long. Though it's too late, I rush from the room and bound onto the landing. Bare feet padding quickly, I can feel Allie's weight work against us. She's bobbing ferociously against my hip as we descend the stairs. I slow to adjust her, losing valuable seconds. The stairs nearly kill me. I see the back door, sunlight streaming through.

A miscalculation.

And I am already cursing myself for what is to come. But I cannot slow down, every nerve in my body is lurching forward, a searing fire inextinguishable, propelling me on. The back door grows closer. I have planned every move that should come next. If we can just make it to the door, if only Allie can see the sun, we can let the wind carry us away from here. We can run forever.

These thoughts calm me. My mind takes refuge in their shade as I shift Allie's weight and grasp the door handle. I swing it open. Bathed in sunlight, morning has come, relief swelling like a gorgeous balloon in my chest.

"And just where do you think you two are going?" A harsh voice yells out from the kitchen. The balloon bursts and the air that rushes inside of me is chaos, a million particles trying to escape. I am deflating, mass is leaving my body, and I almost drop Allie.

"Outside," I manage to mumble.

"And who told you that you could do that?" came the demand.

"No one."

"Come in here where I can see you!"

Reluctantly, I drag myself to the doorway of the kitchen. I feel Allie's dead weight hanging on my hip, clinging on to me, fear pulsing like a current through our skins. I look down at my feet, at the floor. My head swells and I feel like I might float away from here.

"Katerina, you better look at me when I'm talking to you."

I want to throw up. The weight of the air particles is trapped in my throat. It is worse than puke, a mass of all my fears, all the horrible realizations brimming and churning. I turn slowly, my leg numb from Allie hugging my body tightly, to look at him. His gaze is fixed on me, daring me to speak, bacon grease dripping down his jowls into his already oily goatee. *Katerina.* He had said like he owned the word, like he owned the world, like he owned me. He stares at us, eyes aflame.

"You will learn who is in charge here. You know you don't go outside or anywhere unless I say it's OK. I'm so damn sick and tired having to deal with your asses." He barks, his voice echoing around the kitchen. "I don't know why I put up with my sister and her bullshit all the time. Dumping you two on my damn doorstep. I'm always left dealing with the fucking messes she makes."

I have to shut him out. His words sicken me; they are something to be ingested, and even after all this time, it still gets to me.

Allie is crying softly and I rub her back lightly, so he doesn't see. He stands violently, shaking the table and knocking his chair into the back counter with a crash.

"Take your sister and go back upstairs. Get dressed and be back here in five minutes."

Limping from Allie's body latched painfully to my side, I manage to escape to the sanctuary of the first step of the stairs leading back up to my room.

Then I hear him snarl, "You forgot to shut the damn door Katerina! Do you think we live in a fucking barn?"

Gingerly sitting Allie down on to the steps, I drag my body back to the door and shut it, feeling the pressure of his gaze anchor into my spine. With the sound of the latch clicking, I lose the dream of the open air, bright sunlight, and the carefree world beyond this place.

"Come on Allie," I whisper quietly and hoist her back up onto my side, ignoring the sharp pains that flare up in protest. As I ascend the staircase, Allie buries her head into my shoulder and wraps her tiny arms around my neck. I keep replaying the scene downstairs over and over in my mind, but I won't let the tears escape my eyes. Absolutely everything has gone wrong. Night after night, I fill our heads with promises that I can never keep.

I sit Allie down on her bed in her room. She looks up at me with her eyes still red from crying, her delicate features marred with a sadness that I didn't know a five-year-old could express.

"I'm so sorry, Allie." She doesn't say anything at all; she just sits there on her bed looking at me, wanting explanations that I don't have. "Hurry up and finish getting dressed Allie. Please. I'll be back in a minute."

"HOW LONG DOES IT TAKE TO PUT SOME DAMN CLOTHES ON?"

We both flinch as his roaring permeates through the walls and I hurry over across the hall to my own bedroom. As I strip off my nightclothes, I dare to let my mind wander. *What if we had made it out this morning? Where would we have gone? Where was there to go? Could I have remembered how to get to the river from here?*

Probably not.

And then I'm suddenly plunged back into the last summer that I had been to the river.

The day was hot, the kind of heat that makes the water evaporate right off the skin. Allie was there. She was only two at the time and sitting on top of some smooth rocks with her feet in the water. Dad was pulling crawdads out of the water and making them zoom around Allie's head like makeshift airplanes. She was giggling and shrieking with laughter as he brought one close to her face, splashing her hands down in the water to show her delight.

"Watch the pinchers!" I remembered yelling but it changed into muffled laughter as Dad covered himself in crawdads. Mom was a little ways down from us, sunning herself on the grassy bank.

I don't really remember when things stopped being perfect, when we stopped being a family. But one beautiful sunny day, we loaded up our little red Chevy with all of Allie's and my things.

"Where are we going?" I asked my mother, but she turned away from me and faced the passenger-side window. "Dad, where are we going?" I asked again, leaning forward between the two front seats on the cup holder console.

"We're going away for a few days," he answered, looking at me in the rearview mirror.

"Are we going to the river?" I questioned, not hiding the eager excitement in my voice. He glanced back into the rearview at me and smiled.

"Now try to lay back and get some rest, it will be a while before we get where we're going." Mom spoke, but her voice was low and tired. Settling back into my seat, I saw Allie already asleep in her car seat and soon, as I watched the many trees and cars whir past my window, I joined her.

My mind blotted the rest of the memory out. It had been a long time since I had thought about that day, the day we came here. After pulling on my oldest pair of jeans and a tee shirt, I improvise by combing my messy hair with my fingers. When I exit my room, I find that Allie is already waiting for me at the top of the steps. She has managed to put herself into a pair of shorts and an eyelet sleeveless top with everything facing the right direction.

"Look at you Allie, you did so good! I can't believe how much of a big girl you are," I say, infusing my words with as much kindness as possible.

"I had a little trouble with the buttons," she admits sheepishly, pointing to her back.

"It's okay, I'll fix it." I walk over to the top of the stairs and finish buttoning the back of her shirt properly. But the increasing sound of thudding footsteps at the bottom of the steps paralyzes me.

"What is this? Fucking dress-up? Get down here. NOW!" Allie looks back at me instinctively, but I shake my head.

"Don't be afraid Allie," I whisper.

"And stop that damn whispering or else."

Two months after my eleventh birthday, Allie was born. I used to tell my mother that Allie was her birthday present to me that year. I loved her from the moment I saw her wriggling around in the nurse's arms. She was the most amazing thing that I had ever seen. My heart melted as the kind nurse placed her small swathed body in my arms.

"Look at you, big sister, you're a natural," she praised and I beamed. I looked up at my mom, lying in her hospital bed so she could see how happy I was, how thankful I was that she had given Allie to me. But mom did not look at us; she was turned over on her side, looking towards the wall. I looked down into Allie's face. It was scrunched and blotchy

A Veil of Shattered Dreams

like the new babies I'd seen on the TV, but there was something more about her. The way her eyes opened and stared at me with wonder, and even though she had only been in the world for a short time, I felt like we bonded instantly, like she was my own baby.

"Give Allie back to the nurse, Kitty. It's time to go home," I heard Dad say and in a blur, Allie was taken from my arms. My heart sank down into my chest, why did they have to take her away? "Say good-night to your mommy, Kitty," Dad said, taking me by the hand to direct me towards the exit.

"Bye, Mommy," I said, but she gave no sign that she had heard me, still facing the wall, her legs pulled up tightly to her chest under the thin covers.

I follow Allie down the steps and into the kitchen. The table is neatly set with two bowls and matching silverware. I glance over to the kitchen pantry and it takes me a second to realize that there is another person standing there. She appears in the corner of the kitchen, the ghost of a woman, her translucent hair blending in against her overtly pale skin.

"Where's the damn oatmeal at?!" I hear him bark and the ghost woman jumps noticeably against the cabinets.

"I—I—I-It's on the stove," the ghost woman manages to say, hardly above a mumble.

"The stove? Why is it still on the fucking stove? Do you expect them to eat it on the burner? Damn it woman, can't you do anything right?" She looks away from him, down at her feet. "Don't just stand there! Get it!" She flinches, taking a few slow steps toward the stove. "Forget it, just fucking forget it. I'll get it. If I want something done around here, I swear I have to do it my damn self." He grabs the pan aggressively off the burner, slopping oatmeal all over the stove.

"Damn it to hell! Look what you made me do!" He screams at her again. "Clean it up. I ask you to do one simple task, cook the oatmeal, and you can't even do that. You're useless."

She looks at him and nods, "I'm sorry, you're right, you're right," she squeaks, looking frantically from him to Allie, to me to try and see what she should do next, trying to make it over to the kitchen sink without incident. Her black eyes catch mine. They are flat and dull.

I caught a fish once down at our crawdad river a few years before Allie was born. Mom stayed in bed that day, she didn't want to talk to anyone and didn't feel like going anywhere. So Dad and I drove

A Veil of Shattered Dreams

up to the river late in the afternoon. It was the only time that I think he was more excited than I was. Helping me hold the rod up and puncturing the worm on the hook for me, he made sure I knew the correct way to hold the pole and reel the line. I watched the worm dangle from the end of the line, writhing around bleeding and pulsing, the perfect bait.

I cast the rod for the first time in my whole life and my father's face beamed with pride as the line whizzed through the air and plunked with a small splash into the creek. We waited and watched the little currents lap at the cork, tugging the line and feeling for a fish. The line gave a sharp jerk against my reel and my heart was racing as I grasped the rod firmly and reeled the line in hard and fast, feeling the weight and pull of the fish work against me. I imagined what its body looked like under the water, snagged on my hook, combating against my strength. Maneuvering the pole, I pulled the line like I had fished my whole life until the fish burst through the surface, flapping and twitching around. I admired its spirit and the fight that it had waged. I was proud, so proud that I had bested this creature.

"It's a bluegill! Be careful because its fins are spiny," Dad warned, but I had already pulled the fish off the hook. I looked at the fish. It was a lot smaller than I expected, only about the length of half of my hand. Looking at the hook, I saw that the worm was still fully intact, still squirming angrily. Then I looked down at the fish and saw that its gills had stopped moving. The tines on the fins had gone down and the fish no longer struggled. It was dead. I looked into its eyes. They were flat and dull. Not even the water droplets reflected anything from the deep dark pupils.

"Let's take a picture!" Dad says excitedly. I hold the bluegill up by the tail so I cannot see into its face. "Smile!" Dad snaps the photo. I can't hold onto the dead fish any longer and I drop it back into water. But it will never swim again.

Its light was gone.

"Now eat!" The clunking of the pot being sat on the table wakes me from the reverie. The ghost woman turns the faucet on and begins soaping up a dishrag to clean up the spilt oatmeal. He has already sat back down in his own chair and gestures for Allie and I to sit down at our designated places. Once we are seated, he begins ladling out big heaving gooey spoonfuls of oatmeal into our bowls. Quickly, to avoid any more conflict, I begin forcing spoonful after spoonful of the thick stuff down my throat. I don't have time to taste, only to swallow. Each bite is a gag that keeps all my thoughts inside and forces me to concentrate on this moment only. The only sounds I hear are the running of the water at the sink and my own spoon clinking against the bowl as I go back for more mouthfuls. A soft voice, barely audible, breaks through my haze.

"But I don't like oatmeal." I look at Allie; her bowl sits in front of her, oatmeal untouched. It takes him a second to realize that she has spoken, but I am already trying to catch her gaze with mine, to distract her or dissuade her from the subject.

"Excuse me?" His voice cuts in loudly, hitting every nerve in my body and sending anxious skitters down my spine. *Why Allie? Why did you have to say that?* In my mind I'm scolding her, wishing I could blot out this scene from happening. Slowly, and never taking his eyes off of Allie, he rises from the table to stand over her. His huge form swallows her little body in shadow.

"You're going to eat your fucking breakfast and you're going to fucking like it!" He roars and

Allie's head tilts back so her little eyes catch the light. They are wide open and shiny, with tears forming in them. "Are you going to be a cry baby? Go ahead little baby and cry. Look everyone, look what we have here, a little baby. Go ahead, cry, you little shit."

"I want Daddy," Allie manages to say as a torrent of tears starts washing down her face.

"Too fucking bad, your daddy left you here with me. He didn't want you. He doesn't love you. So go ahead and cry, little baby." My heart shatters. Allie looks at me, sobbing and shaking her head, not believing anything that he is telling her.

"What, you don't believe me? You think *she* will tell you any different?" He points at me and laughs. "Go ahead Katerina, tell her. Tell her! Let's see if you know whether Daddy and Mommy give a shit about the pair of you."

Everything that is reservoired inside my heart bursts wide open, like a lake overflowing its dam. I'm unable to block the memory from rushing through me, the first day here washing over me again in a flood.

A Veil of Shattered Dreams

When I woke, it was still daylight. As I glanced out the window, I didn't recognize any of the scenery around us.

"Daddy, where are we?" I asked. "When are we going to get to the river?"

"We're almost there, okay?" he said, but his voice was quieter than before and he sounded worn. I looked over at Allie. She was still sleeping, rocking gently with the movement of her car seat. We pulled up to an old-looking farmhouse on the side of the road. The house was average sized, but much in need of repairs. Some shingles had been blown off and not replaced. The driveway was broken up from where the pavement had weathered over time. There was a small flowerbed outside the front windows, which made it look like the house could have been someone's home, but stubby weeds had overtaken it. A covered porch jutted out from the side of the house. A small driveway led away from the porch and wound in front of the house to meet the road. Dad parked the car on the shoulder of the road. He climbed out and went around to the trunk.

"Where are we?" I asked, but nobody answered me. I didn't know whether Mom was awake, so I climbed up halfway onto the console to look at her.

She was awake, but only just. She was staring out the window again, her gaze fixated on the old house.

"Mom," I asked, "What is this place? Why are we stopping here? I thought we were supposed to go to the river." She was silent. Suddenly, I heard Dad tapping on my window, beckoning me to get out. I opened the car door slowly and crawled out. I heard the car door slam on the other side as Dad pulled Allie from her car seat.

The house sat alone on a vast stretch of road where fields surrounded it on both sides. Our car was the only vehicle that that seemed to know that this house existed here. I walked over to my father and he clasped my hand in his. Allie was situated in his other arm and he walked us around onto the driveway and up onto the porch.

"Dad," I asked nervously because we had never been to this place before, "what are we doing here? What is this place?" He didn't say a word, but strode in front of me to knock on the door. We waited a few seconds, and then a man appeared at the threshold. He looked at Dad and then surveyed Allie and me. I reached out to grab Allie by the hand.

A Veil of Shattered Dreams

"Is this everything then?" he asked and Dad nodded.

"Dad, what's going on?" I demanded. A strange sense of fear hung over me.

"This is your Uncle, you remember your mom's brother, girls? This is his home." The man in the doorframe shifted and rolled his eyes. I decided that I already did not like our "Uncle".

"So, what are we doing here?" I asked again, still holding on to Allie's hand.

"Oh," Dad said suddenly, never looking at Allie or me, "I forgot the camera." He started back towards the car, and I saw him nod again at our Uncle. He inclined his head at Allie and me and said, "Wait here a second, okay?"

"Dad," I protested, but he was already heading back to the car. I stared up at the man standing in the doorframe. He was the complete opposite of our mother. His eyes and hair were inky black and he had a little goatee on his chin. He said nothing, but continued to look out towards where my father had gone.

Out on the road, I heard the car engine roar to life. I craned my neck around the porch just quick enough to see the Chevy start pulling away.

"Dad?!" I yelled after him, half shouting, half questioning. Then by the door, I noticed what I had not noticed before. Allie's and mine's small suitcases were piled neatly against the house. Instinctively, I leapt from the porch.

"D-AAAAA-D!" I screamed, " COME BACK! WHERE ARE YOU GOING? DAD!" A thousand realizations slammed into me and took my breath away, but I fought through it and began to run.

"DADDY, PLEASE!" I shouted, trailing the little red car by an impossible distance. My vision blurred in a stream of tears, but I kept running blindly after the car.

A rock tangled up my feet and I fell, hitting the hard asphalt, knocking the life out of my chest. And then it was like I wasn't anywhere, like I was hovering over my body, watching myself from above.

"TELL HER!" He roars and a jolt pulses through me, ripping me violently from the memory. It takes me a second to realize that I am crying too. I look over at Allie and am rifled with a guilt that seemed absent from our parents.

"STOP!" I yell directly at him. His head jerks to me.

"Excuse me? What did you just say? WHAT THE FUCK DID YOU JUST SAY TO ME?"

"Stop!" I cry out again, somewhere between a shout and a gasp.

Another mistake. As soon as the words leave my lips, my stomach cringes. I slide off the chair and try to make a mad dash to the stairs.

"You ungrateful little bitch!" I hear his chair scrape against the floor again and clatter into the counter. My head start saves me. I scramble up the steps and into my room, hearing his thundering footsteps right behind me.

I dive into my bed, rolling up in the sheets, and bury my nose in them. Breathing in their comforting scents, my heart is sputtering. I plead silently, *please make it go away.*

The footsteps stop right outside my door, but it doesn't open. Instead, the jingling of keys and a series of small clicks lets me know that I'm locked in.

I let out a small sob. Two years. Two years, we've been here and they've never been back once. *Oh Daddy, I miss you so much. Why did you have to leave us here alone?* I let out a sob and the tears start to well up in my eyes. I cannot keep the anger and the devastating sorrow from flooding my heart. My head is spinning and my mind lifts out of my body and fills up with feelings that I don't understand. I let out a slight scream and listen to it reverberate in my ears. *Go ahead Katerina, tell her. Tell her!* The words bounce around and beat themselves against my skull. The ceiling is coming down on top of me, crushing my body and pressing the breath from my lungs. Then I am fading. Darkness wraps its comforting arms around me and lures me into sweet unconsciousness.

Leon

Soaring. That's what dreaming is like. It's falling without design, but without fear. Without fail. Soaring through a sea of black and every color imaginable until everything is white. The dream morphs before my eyes and the blurry edges solidify into white walls. My body rearranges itself into form and I find it odd that I am still lying down. My head spins because everything that was once blessedly out of focus is now sharpening rapidly before my eyes.

Looking around, I wonder at first if I am awake because I see that the room resembles my bedroom with blank walls. But this room has two windows. Sunlight is streaming in from the smaller one near my bed and the other one is large, next to a door which looks out into a busy hallway.

Something is different, the weight of the air, the extra heaviness of my breath. I don't seem to be in my bedroom; my bed is gone, replaced with a stiff white quilt on a metal frame. *What is this place?*

Voices and sounds slice crisply into my calm. It plunges me into a vivid awareness. I turn my head to the noise and, through the open door, see that the scene is alive with sound and the haze of people rushing around. Turning my head back to the other side, I am unnerved to see that I am not alone. He is sleeping and snoring rather loudly.

I look down at my feet, rise, and plant them firmly but quietly on the floor. Tiptoeing around the bed, I slowly creep up on him. *Who is he?* I scan over his handsome features, prominent facial bones pressing against sleek dark skin. It occurs to me ironically that he is sleeping in *my* dream and I begin to laugh out loud. Startled awake, he falls to the floor with a crash. He stares up at me from the floor.

"Who are you?" I demand sharply, the words coming out more hostile than I intend. "What are you doing here?"

Reaching for the chair, he uses it to pull himself up from the floor. He looks intently at me and his eyes seize my body from the inside out. They are penetratingly blue, odd given the dark color of his skin, and I can't help but find them interesting.

Apprehensively, I repeat, "Who are you?" but when I ask it, it is quieter, almost kind. In that moment, it is more than a formality or a pleasantry; it's a need. We lock eyes, searching each other for answers to our own unspoken questions.

He breaks the gaze first and looks down sheepishly.

"I'm Leon, remember?" he says, turning his gaze back to me. He stands a few inches above me. His height intimidates me a little and he is standing so close that his chest is right next to my face. I should pull away, every nerve is telling me to keep my distance from this strange person, but I'm frozen. He eases around my frozen body and walks over to the open door to survey the commotion happening outside the room and then turns back to me.

"Now that you're up, I was thinking that you might wanna try and sneak out to the courtyard today?" he suggests, eyes twinkling mischievously under the fluorescents. In this unfamiliar room, in this unfamiliar place, I'm at a loss for words. But he seems kind, like a person that you could inherently trust, with his gentle smile and tone. I want to follow him, intrigued by his appearance, and glad that I am not alone. Mesmerized, I nod and cautiously walk towards him, afraid any sudden movement might jolt me awake and I will be ripped away from this curious stranger. A courtyard? That sounded nice, a lot nicer than where I had come from.

Then I think about Allie and how she seems so far away from me. Actually, everything seems so far away, the cursing and the taunting, the paralyzing fear. Those emotions bubble around me, but the surface tension holds steadfast.

Unexpectedly, he clasps ahold of my elbow. The movement is so sinuous, that I gaze up at him in surprise. He leads me out of the room and into the hallway traffic. People whiz past, heading from one end of the building to the other. Some are pushing others in wheelchairs and some, like Leon and I, are heading toward the main doors. Avoiding anything but our destination, we weave through the sea of people drifting in front of the door. Voices and people melt into each other, overlapping in the din. We speed up and the doors grow bigger and my legs tingle with their swift new pace, unhindered by the weight of a clinging child.

As we approach the doors, my pulse quickens. They are heavy and bolted. My nerves hyper activate once again, the anxious emotions coursing through my veins. Leon reaches the doors before I do and begins to push the bolt aside. Slivers of sunlight burst through the cracks around the door, and I can sense their warmth, their organic tendrils of happiness.

"Leon! Where are you going?" calls someone from a distance. We halt suddenly. Leon anxiously turns towards the voice. I wince; the fear is growing again. The door is so close. I can almost imagine the scene beyond.

"Everything's under control. Don't worry, Mrs. Babbitt," Leon responds and faces back to me, waving her off.

"Take care, Leon. Remember your responsibilities! And don't stay out too long!" her voice echoes down the hallway.

He sees my confused expression and pats my arm reassuringly. "Don't worry about Mrs. Babbitt. She's always worried about something."

He smiles and the warmth spreads through his face as he pushes the door open. And then we're bathed in the glorious sun.

Dreams are so beautiful because they show you that you are capable of obtaining anything you desire. And I desired more than anything in this moment to drink in the sunlight. To let the light breeze ripple through my hair. To stand under the sky and not be afraid.

"It's a nice day out," Leon comments and I nod vigorously. He sets us on a path following a meandering grey cement sidewalk. Ahead of us, there is a small garden. "I thought we could sit in the courtyard for a while. I'm sure it's nice for you to be outside for a change," he says, reading my thoughts.

The courtyard is flanked by bright green hedges on both sides with spurts of pink roses entwined in them. Past the gate, an arbor arches overhead with tufts of ivy vines clustered and winding through it. We walk under the arbor and into the grassy yard. The courtyard is one of the loveliest places I've ever seen. I'm reminded of our crawdad creek and how places take up as much space in my heart as people.

A Veil of Shattered Dreams

"Katerina! There you are!" I hear Dad yelling from behind me. His voice is on the edge of panic and relief. I say nothing to acknowledge him, but stare down into my own reflection in the water.

"Come on honey, it's time to leave." I don't want to go.

"Can't we just stay here?" I ask wistfully and I hear Dad's soft chuckle behind me and feel his hand rest on my shoulder.

"Kitty Kat, I would love nothing more than to stay here with you."

"Then why do we have to go?" I ask, splashing one of my bare feet into the creek. It was so lovely here. With the cool water washing over the silty bank and cattails shooting up with the wildflowers near the shore, creating an overlapping sanctuary. The sun was just settling down over the low lying hills and rays of orange diffused over the rocks and through the river grass.

"Baby, your mommy needs us. But we can always come back. I promise. This can be our special place. No matter what happens, no matter whom we bring here, this will always be ours. It's magic."

"Really?"

"Really really. The magic keeps it like this forever, so that it stays beautiful even in the rain or in the snow, or even hundreds of years from now. But if we stay too long, we make the magic run out. Then everything will dry out and the creek will run dry and we won't be able to come here ever again."

"But I don't want it to die!" I cry and turn around to face him, terror on my face.

"We'll come back, and next time maybe Mommy and your new baby sister can both come with us. Don't you think they'd love it here too?" His arm wraps around my shoulder and pulls me in to kiss the top of my head. "If we let the magic build up, maybe we can stay for two days instead of just an afternoon." I nod my head vigorously. Dad smiles as he walks me back toward the car.

My vision swims in front of me as Leon and the courtyard come back into focus. Crawdad Creek still lingers in the back of my thoughts, now swarming with nostalgia. We haven't been there in years and I can only imagine how wonderful it must be now. Then I'm reminded of Allie; I wish so much that she could be here with me, so she could experience the magic too. These thoughts sadden me a little and it must show because Leon squeezes my arm and inquires kindly, "Is something wrong?"

"No," a bit untruthful, not wanting to share my thoughts, "Everything is wonderful."

In the center of the courtyard, I spy a wrought iron bench taking refuge in the shade of an oak, whose leaves have exploded into a web of green. I point to the bench, but Leon is already heading toward it. Hungrily I look around, trying to drink in the beauty of the garden, burning it to memory. I inhale its magic, just enough to preserve this moment. My brain latches on to every detail and I feel like I've been here before. It's like the scene jars me to try and recreate it from memory. But then I get lost, as if something is stopping me from accessing it. Leon sits down on the bench and gestures for me to sit next to him. A butterfly flutters onto his hand.

"It's beautiful," I say, admiring the span of its black and purple wings resting on the back of his hand.

"It didn't used to be as beautiful," Leon explains, watching it take off into the air. "Once it was a caterpillar, one with high hopes for the future."

"Metamorphosis is a wonderful thing. But one never knows what the future holds," I state logically and inhale the crisp air deeply. *How long will I be allowed to stay here?* I puzzle, still trying to make sense of where I am. How long before I'm torn away, back into my bedroom? Where the sun doesn't exist for me.

"It's a long winding road that you're on," Leon remarks knowingly after a while. "The journey is going to be difficult. But I can help you, if you want," he suggests cryptically. "That's why I'm here."

"Thank you for bringing me here," I say, not totally understanding what he's offering. Then I think about what awaits me when I wake. In the recesses of my mind, I can feel a darkness gathering and I pull my knees up into my chest.

Suddenly everything is too harsh. The sun is burning into my back, the air too dense to breathe. The green of the garden is overloading my senses. How long have I been gone? It feels like hours, and I begin to worry about Allie again. And with the thought of her, the darkness weaves itself deeper into my mind.

"You're welcome," Leon replies. Somehow he senses my withdrawal and asks, "How are you feeling?"

"Fine," I lie, pulling more into myself.

"It's okay. You can tell me anything. You can trust me," Leon asserts gently, sliding closer to me on the bench.

"But I don't even know you," I interject forcefully, sliding away from him. Every sense is ablaze, encouraging me to trust this stranger, to trust this projection of my own mind to see me through. There is something in the way he is looking at me that I cannot decipher. A hint of frustration?

"But you do know me," he insists and his bright eyes fill me up with peace.

There is so much that I want to say that I feel he won't understand. But then I don't want to say anything at all; I just want to run back into the sweet nothingness of unconscious sleep.

"Katerina," he pleads, his tone losing its careful composure. He knows my name.

"You know my name?" I'm surprised but he presses on, ignoring my question.

"It's me, Leon." He touches my hand, softly searching my face for something that he seems not able to find.

"Can we go inside?" I ask anxiously, pulling my hand away. Leon lets out a deep sigh, exhaling greatly.

"I'll take you inside," he concedes, disappointment heavy in his voice as we stand up from the bench. He clears his throat and inclines his head like he wants to say something else, but he doesn't.

Will I ever see him again? He seems so substantial, like his impression is already molded into my subconscious. I worry that I might not ever see this place again, that I might not remember any of it. A cloud of anxiety is condensing, adding to the darkness. Leon takes my elbow again and that firm but gentle grasp is just enough to ground me here a little longer.

"I know everything seems a little scary right now. It's okay to feel lost." His voice resumes the calm and caring façade that I recognize as we leave the courtyard.

And I do feel lost. Lost in this strange familiar dream that has me anchored here. Memories pool in the back of my mind, ready to spill their contents, to offer me an explanation or wake me up. Do I already have a memory of this dream? Have I dreamed of this place, of Leon before? I reach for the memory and try to hold on to its dissipating form, but it slips out of my grasp.

"Katerina," Leon's voice invades my thoughts. "Are you alright?" I realize that I must look a million miles away, trapped by my own ruminations. But even outside of sleep, outside the kindness of closed eyes and unconscious bliss, I am trapped. And I know as soon as I wake, I will be lost again inside my Uncle's house, never knowing how to escape.

As we walk back to the main doors, I let my mind wander. I must be close to waking up, I think. Only barely aware of my steps, I walk beside Leon. Everything is beginning to blur, with patches of dark swirling into my vision. People are coming outside now and the world is slowing down as they brush past us. All the extra movement is starting to throw me off balance, so I stop to steady myself.

"Katerina?" Leon turns to see me, but his voice sounds like it is at the end of a tunnel. As I stand in the middle of the sidewalk, I feel reality split itself in two. My uncle's ghost woman is gliding toward me. Her eyes are focused only on her destination. She is almost transparent in the sun and I brace myself for the frightening voice I know will follow her. She passes me without taking notice of who I am or where we are. I want to say something to her but I can't make my mouth work, like I've misplaced my tongue. The threatening voice does not come. Not yet.

"Come on, please, we're almost back." Leon's voice urges, registering distantly in my ears. Suddenly, the darkness breaks through into my thoughts, taking control of my body. I forget how to walk, how to even form a single thought. My knees sway and my body lurches forward, unbalanced. Somehow I remain upright and with Leon's support, I make it back inside the building and onto the strange bed.

Inside is only a ribbon of color, light, and sound as the woman called Mrs. Babbitt asks anxiously, "Leon! What happened to her?"

"You're okay now," he soothes me and then turns to Mrs. Babbitt. "Let me explain."

"I trusted you, Leon, and then *this* happens," she interrupts. Leon starts to speak again but I can't make out his words. I am aware of him for only another instant and that I may never see him again. The room is swallowed by black.

Plans

Waking up has never felt like this before. I open my eyes and the after-images still dance in front of my sight. I'm lying wide-awake in my own bed and thinking about all that has just happened. My bedroom feels dull and flat in comparison to my vivid memories of the dream. A trapping sensation weaves itself above my bed, preventing me from going back to sleep.

The memory of Leon's face pushes to the front of my thoughts. Whoever he is, he had seemed to really care about me. I am thankful that my mind is capable of creating such a kind individual. The sun had been such a blessing, my hope fulfilled. All these new memories of the outside, of the courtyard, remind me that the world can actually be wonderful beyond this place. Then, I remember Allie. I promised her Crawdad Creek. I promised her better than this life.

A Veil of Shattered Dreams

I rise from my bed and it feels like I have been asleep for hours. Stepping across the room, I pull the door open, and go out into the hallway. Everything is so strangely quiet. Light peaks up from the downstairs into the hall. It is still daylight. I creep along the rough threadbare carpet to the top of the stairs. The dilapidated grandfather clock begins to chime at the foot of the stairs. Ten times. Ten o'clock. I've only been asleep for an hour. Uncle will be gone by now. He always leaves for work around nine-thirty every work morning. Cautiously, I descend the steps.

"Kitty!" I hear a shriek and then something slams hard against my body, knocking the air from my lungs.

"Calm down Allie, I'm here." I say, sitting down on the steps and trying to catch my breath. "What happened after I left? Was Uncle really mad?" Allie nods. She doesn't elaborate and I don't ask anything else.

"How did you get down here?" Allie interjects.

"What do you mean..." I begin, and then I remember the cruel sharp click of Uncle locking me in my room this morning.

"Uncle said he locked you up," Allie insists.

"I *was* locked up," I say, "but when I woke up, the door was unlocked."

"Weird." She grows quiet and crawls up onto my lap.

"I'm sorry about this morning," I murmur into her ear. "It was my fault. I should have planned better."

"Are we ever going to get out of here?"

"It's only the start of the summer. You'll go to school this year."

"That's not what I mean. I miss Daddy."

"I know. I'm trying Allie. I really am trying. But I need you to help me. Can you do that?" Allie nods vigorously into my chest. "Come up to my room after you finish your chores, okay?" She nods again. "I've got to stay up there and pretend like I'm still locked up or they'll know. Understand?" I explain. Allie scoots off my lap and scampers back into the kitchen. I turn around and climb back up the stairs to my prison.

It couldn't have been past ten-thirty, as the grandfather clock has not chimed again, when I hear footsteps coming up the hallway. I lean against the paint chipped wooden door, straining to listen for any clues to who might be outside. Thud. Thunk. Thud. Thunk. The footsteps stop right outside my door. My insides freeze and I propel myself as quietly and quickly as I can on tip-toe back to the bed. Pulling the sheet back over my body, I close my eyes and pretend that I am asleep. The lock clicks and the knob turns slowly.

"Well I'll be damned!" screeches a disapproving female voice, "She was right. You *are* still in bed." I recognize her voice and it fills me with dread. "Get up." Even with my eyes closed, I can sense her coming over to the bed. She rips the sheet away from me and tosses it to the floor. "Clean this mess up. This place is a disgrace. My poor son goes out and works his ass off every morning providing for you, and then I come here and see you ingrates lounging around like there aren't things to be done."

I'd forgotten it was grocery day. Rolling out of bed, I hastily bend down to retrieve the sheet off the floor. *It's nice to see you too, Grams,* I say to myself as I hastily make the bed. Gramma Eva is the only thing we ever had that might resemble a grandmother. She is my mom and uncle's mother who has always hated having a daughter. A fact that she never lets us forget.

"You look absolutely terrible, Katerina. When was the last time you combed your hair? Have a little pride for heaven's sake. Your mother is already a dreadful reflection on me. We don't need to continue down that line, do we?" she chastises, hands on her hips, and eyes glaring at me. She is severe looking, with heavily lidded eyes and a permanent scowl etched in her aging face like some garish gargoyle. She might have once been pretty, but something has poisoned her beauty, leaving a wicked gaze in its place. The ghost woman appears at the door, Allie trotting right up behind her.

"Time for us to go," Gramma Eva announces, but the ghost woman says nothing. Aggravated with her non-response, Gramma sweeps dramatically past them into the hall. The ghost woman increases her steps to catch up with Gramma as Allie falls back to walk with me. Gramma stops suddenly and turns to the ghost woman to survey her.

"Why my son chose to marry a wretch like you, I will never know," she declares, grasping the ghost woman's chin in her hand and looking directly into her empty black eyes. "It's a shame you aren't more attractive. That might excuse your careless disregard for the way things look around this place." She gestures her arms around to the recently vacuumed hallway and freshly shined wooden banister. "Filth!" Shaking her head, she walks on to the end of the hallway and disappears down the steps with the ghost woman trailing after. Allie and I follow close behind. The wooden banister gleams brightly in the dim daylight and I suddenly have a vision of Gramma Eva tripping on the stairs and tumbling down each of the ghost woman's meticulously polished steps. But I let it subside.

When I was only a little bit older than Allie is now, my parents left me over at Gramma's house one night while they went out for the evening. Reluctantly, and not without argument, I found myself sitting alone and uncomfortable in one of her stiff chintz armchairs. The air had been pervadingly stale, unsuccessfully masked by the strong odor of cheap perfume that reminded me of rotting rose bushes. All the furniture and décor was pristine, but out of another time. As much as she had wished, she could never prevent the subtle, natural aging of things. It was absolutely terrifying and empty, but Gramma had prided herself on its immaculateness as soon as I made it across the threshold.

Rachel Stark

"Now, don't touch anything. I didn't spend all my time cleaning the place for some grimy urchin to put their little hands on everything," she ordered tersely. Her bony hands, perched on the back of my shoulders, steered me into the perfectly preserved sitting room. I imagined her scrubbing and scrubbing away all the warmth and life out of the walls. She herself was the emulation of it, polished but cold, and already dead inside.

I take Allie's hand and we start to descend the staircase side-by-side. Halfway down the stairs, I pick up Gramma Eva's bitter tone as she continues to hound the ghost woman. "You don't have the list?! Then go get it! It's not like I haven't got other things to do today." She sighs pretentiously, tapping her foot against the carpet. The ghost woman darts quickly into the kitchen and makes a beeline to where she left the paper. Allie and I climb down the rest of the steps and into the lower hallway. It is narrow, lined with nubby coarse carpeting that forces your feet to scuff against it while you walk. Looking into the kitchen, I see the ghost woman pause suddenly upon reaching the stove. She grabs a cleaning rag and begins to wipe away a barely-there smudge.

A Veil of Shattered Dreams

"Why are you taking so damn long?" Gramma Eva asks impatiently and pushes past me and Allie into the kitchen. "It's too late. You're too late. Just give me your shopping list," she demands in increasing exasperation, yanking the cleaning rag and the list from the ghost woman's grip.

The ghost woman hurries by us, her eyes focused only on her destination – the front door. Simultaneously, the ghost woman and I move to dodge each other as I pull Allie aside and squish our bodies against the wall to allow the ghost woman to pass. The memory of my morning dream surfaces instantly and I remember the bright sun and her translucent figure gliding toward me. I stop suddenly in the hall and watch her as the vivid residue of that other world freezes me in this moment.

Then I catch my reflection in the wall mirror on the opposite side of the hallway. It is hard to remember the last time I looked into a mirror, but I am pretty sure that this is the first time I look and see a stranger. The girl staring back at me doesn't look like the person I remember.

Once my father had told me how much I had looked like my mother, but I didn't believe him.

Rachel Stark

Our mother used to be beautiful, with strong features and defined cheekbones. She always looked like some exotic princess, or well she did until very recently. When I remember her now, all I can imagine is that poison carved into her face exactly like her mother's. That poison which latched onto her and injected itself into her bones and penetrated all the way down into her spirit. But unlike Gramma Eva, my mother did not master it. She succumbed to it.

In the mirror, I see the same faint proclivities beginning to form. Under wistful eyes with faded grey irises, the tangible evidence of a young woman whose soul has left her a long time ago. Skin pallid with gaunt hollowed cheeks, empty recesses where rosy happiness used to reside. All gone. A long thin scar is clearly visible over my left eyebrow. An accident, or rather an act of stupidity on my part. It is the only physical scar on my body and I couldn't even blame my uncle for it. Those scars run deeper, invisible to the naked eye. The sight is nauseating and I want to reach up and shatter the image in the mirror into a thousand pieces.

A Veil of Shattered Dreams

Another reflection suddenly appears beside me in the mirror, surprisingly similar, but crueler, and interrupts my thoughts.

"Vanity is so unbecoming of you Katerina, and what a waste. Trust me, no one will want to bother even giving you a second look," Gramma Eva scorns cruelly. "Here, take this," she says, tossing me the cleaning rag. "You might try to be decent at something, though it wouldn't surprise me if you didn't." She continues, "Your mother was the same way. The one great disappointment in my life. And then she went and burdened her hardworking brother with the likes of you two." She jerks her head down towards Allie and scoffs, "Grubby little beggars. I would have taken you to the group home had someone left you on *my* doorstep." I almost reply, *I would have much rather gone to a group home than stay here in this underworld*, but I remain silent.

I watch as Gramma picks her purse up off its usual resting place on the floor and swings it over her shoulder. She reaches down into its depths, hand searching for something. Out of the bag, she pulls a gleaming set of jangling keys. Something about them ignites a response inside of me, like I am aware of them for the first time. They dangle and clink against each other as she picks the one she wants. I notice a skinnier silver key with a black rubber head and recognize it instantly as an ignition key to a vehicle. She holds it against her palm as a second key; a wider, all silver one is grasped in her skeletal fingers. I look over at Allie and she too is staring at the keys, her little eyes spellbound by their shininess.

"I'm locking you in again," she says. "We shouldn't be gone more than an hour or so. I want the whole banister wiped down and shined, all the appliances gleaming when we get home." She must notice our faces, but she thinks we're staring at the door. She pushes Allie and me out from in front of her, joining the ghost woman toward the exit. She unlocks the double cylinder deadbolt from the inside and opens the door wide enough to allow herself and the ghost woman through. She pulls it shut with a deafening bang and we hear her fumble the key around in the jamb until the outside lock clicks.

Allie looks up at me, her tiny little eyes now round and enormous.

"Did you see all those keys that she has?" Allie asks, excitement audible in her voice. "They're so pretty!"

"Yes, I did," I reply, also a little enthusiastic but for a different reason. "Do you know if she leaves her purse by the door every grocery day?"

"Umm," Allie begins, "I think so, umm, I know she doesn't like to carry it around because umm, she always likes to show Auntie what to do. I think it gets in her way." Allie explains, her excitement buzzing. My brain is scheming a million miles an hour and I look into her wide eyes, hoping that she will go along with another one of my plans.

"Do you still want to try and leave here with me one day? Do you still want to go to the creek?" Allie's excitement weakens slightly and she looks a little nervously back at me. I know that she is recalling the morning's horrific events.

"Do you trust me?" I ask, quieter and softer than before, needing her to cooperate. She nods slowly.

"Okay, the next grocery day is one week from today. That means that for the next few days, I need you to help me gather some supplies, okay?" Allie nods in agreement. "Because next grocery day, while Gramma is upstairs helping Auntie, you're going to go downstairs and sneak those pretty keys from Gramma's purse."

I look directly into Allie's eyes to make sure that she understands me. "And then I'm going to meet you at the front door with our stuff, but we've got to be very quiet, okay?" Allie shakes her head up and down, jiggling with impatience. "Once you have her keys, we can sneak outside and lock them inside. Then, I'll start up Gramma's car and then…"

"And then we can go find Daddy!" Allie finishes excitedly.

"Yes," I concede, not wanting to distract or upset her. "Then we can go find Daddy. But you can't say anything okay? Not a word. I want to make sure that we are far away by the time they realize we're gone."

"I get it, Kitty," Allie replies more like a fifteen-year-old than a five-year-old. But then a dark cloud spreads across her face. "Do you really think it will work this time?"

"What other options do we have? School's out, so there's no way to talk to anyone from there. We don't have a telephone and Uncle has the only cell phone in the house, so we can't call anyone. We don't have a computer, so we can't get on the internet…" I answer, listing the possible means to plan a different kind of escape attempt.

"I get it, Katerina," Allie says in irritation, surprising me with her adult attitude.

"So are you going to help me or not?"

"Yeah."

"Good. Now let's start getting things together," I say and turn to go back down the hallway to the stairs.

"But wait!" Allie calls and I turn back to her.

"What?"

"Do you even know how to drive?"

I smile, shrugging off her question and continuing on my way to the top of the steps.

That evening after Gramma finally leaves, (having invited herself to dinner) and after Allie and I washed the dishes, Uncle sends us straight up to bed. I am surprised that this night passed without incident. In my room, I finally feel as though things might be looking up for Allie and me.

I don't dream of Leon again. Not this night. I lay awake for hours thinking about the plan that Allie and I had come up with earlier that day. It seems like a good plan, as correcting and reprimanding the ghost woman easily distracts Gramma. But in order for it to all work out, there is no room for any more errors on my part

It isn't until the very next evening after another ordeal of a day (Allie broke a plate by accident after dinner) that I am finally able to go to my room. Under my bed, I have been storing some items that I want to take with us when Gramma comes next week. I have only managed to nab Allie and mine's winter coats from the downstairs closet and a ragged old blanket from the linen closet so far without detection. It is a start. As I lay in the bed, I wonder if this plan might actually work itself out, but my heart is afraid of hoping. Hope is my best ally and my worst enemy, capable of masking out the bad times with dreams and wishes, but also capable of shattering them in the same moment. I close my eyes, trying to hold onto the hope, and then I am here no more.

Anchored

When I open my eyes again, I am pleasantly surprised to see the same room where I first met Leon. Although, as I look around, I realize that I am alone. In the back of my mind, I am a bit troubled and I begin wondering where Leon is, if he is even here. I rise up from the bed and begin to walk around the room. There are a few things that I never noticed before. There is a little ledge at the bottom of the large glass window next to the door with several picture frames sitting on it. I wonder if they had been there the last time, but I cannot remember.

Intrigued, I make my way over to the ledge to examine the picture frames.

They all contain photos of people. They all look vaguely familiar, like I've seen them or met them before, but no names come to mind except for one person in the photos. It sits behind all the others and I scoot them out of the way to pick it up. It's of Allie and me. We look incandescently happy. She's sitting on my lap outside in the grass and I am giving her a soft kiss on the cheek. She's smiling so radiantly back at me, and for a second, I am overwhelmed with a wave of deep sadness, but I'm not able to understand it.

"You didn't have your scar then," a familiar male voice interjects from behind me. I jump back, startled, and almost drop the frame. It's Leon. I turn around to face him, clutching the frame to my chest. "I'm sorry," he says, seeing my expression, "I didn't mean to startle you."

"It's okay," I say, looking back at the picture in my hands. "And you're right, I didn't."

His hand reaches out, pointing at the picture. "Your sister?" he inquires and I notice a hint of melancholy in his voice. I nod and place the frame back on to the ledge, but continue to look at it. Drawing me out of my stare, Leon asks, "How are you feeling today?"

His face resumes his usual mood of chipperness. I say nothing and just stare at him. I'm back here and Leon is here and the realization of everything that happened last time I was here hits me so fresh. I see him watching my face, analyzing every expression I make.

"Thank you for taking me outside," I say sincerely and the words say more, the unspoken thanks of him helping me back inside. "I'm sure at the end I must have scared you."

Leon smiles. "Only just a bit. You seem better today."

"I feel better."

"Well, that's great to hear!" comes a booming female voice from the doorway. She is tall and matronly looking, holding a small plastic cup full of multi-colored pills and a glass of water.

"Med time!" Turning her pleasant round face toward me, she gestures me over to her. "Come now, Katerina dear, I've got other things I've got to do today."

"What are they for?" I ask, eyeing the little pills. "Why do I need to take pills?"

"She's only been up for a few minutes, Mrs. Babbitt." Leon explains, looking at her like he is trying to convey his thoughts through his eyes. Turning to me, Leon answers my question, "They're so you don't get light-headed again."

"Your meds, dear," she insists, holding the medicine and glass out encouragingly toward me and I take them from her.

"But I feel fine," I object. Gently, I feel the soft pressure of Leon's hand resting on my arm. The gesture is unexpected, but kind. A reassuring warmth surges from his hand into my arm.

"Go ahead and take them," Leon's voice is soft and encouraging. Trustingly, I nod and dump the cup of pills in my mouth, washing them down with the cool water. Smiling, Mrs. Babbitt looks over at Leon almost endearingly.

"She's making quite the progress, and we only just recently lowered the dosage," Mrs. Babbitt shares with him.

"Making progress with what?" I interject, confused with the whole situation.

"Do you think she's ready to be re-introduced today?" Leon asks hopefully.

"It looks very promising," Mrs. Babbitt agrees and nods her head in approval at Leon.

I look at both of them perplexed; I don't understand anything that's happening. Leon says nothing and nods back at Mrs. Babbitt. Then he turns his head to me and smiles his infectious bright smile. I smile back, I can't help it, and for the first time in a long time, I feel like I am supposed to be here in this moment.

"Remember to have her down at the activity room in fifteen minutes for her re-introduction. Sanjay will be so happy to see how well she is doing." Mrs. Babbitt interrupts the moment. Taking the little empty cup and glass from me, she leaves, prattling on about the rest of the things on her to-do list. After she is out of the room, I clasp a hold of Leon's wrist. The movement surprises him and I am met with his wide eyes. I don't say anything, but he understands my confusion and my need to hold onto something and doesn't pull away.

"Why do we have to go to the activity room? What are we going to be doing in there?" I ask.

"You sure do ask a lot of questions," Leon observes, kidding with me for the first time.

"This is *my* dream, but I always feel like everyone knows something I don't. I'm supposed to be in charge here."

"Hey now, baby steps there. We don't need another repeat of last time." And I remember now how my last visit here ended. I blame sensory overload; it had been too much too soon. My excitement of going outside mixed with all the new sights and sounds were too much for my mind to handle at once. Even with my light-headedness, it had been a beautiful dream. I grin at him sheepishly which causes him to grin too because we both are remembering my near-collapse on the sidewalk. I look at him, dark skin in a nice contrast with his white t-shirt and khaki pants, eyes sparkling.

"I'm really glad you're here." I say truthfully, stepping in closer to him, happy to have someone helping me navigate these weird dreams.

"I'm here for you," he replies softly.

"What's in the activity room?" I repeat my earlier question, releasing Leon's wrist now that I feel more grounded.

"It's just a quick session with Sanjay and the others. It shouldn't take more than an hour."

"An hour? I can't stay that long. I've got to get back. They'll notice if I'm gone for too long," I say apprehensively, thinking of Allie back at home, probably curled up next to me, waiting for me to wake up.

Leon nods indulgently at me as I fluff some of my pillows. My gaze follows him as he straightens a faded painting hanging above my bed and I notice that the walls are not bare after all. The painting is of some wildflowers and the curtains for the big glass window are billowy and lavender colored. I had not taken the time to notice them before.

"I promise it won't be too long. You only have to stay as long as you want."

"Okay," I agree reluctantly.

"Okay, then let's go. Or you know Mrs. Babbitt will come back in here and fuss at us." He starts over to the door and I follow.

"Come on slowpoke, you're going to make us late," he jokes and I smile back.

It has been a long time since someone's joked with me or made me smile and I start to remember how much I like to laugh. I meet Leon at the door, but happen to glance around him and catch my reflection in the big glass window. I am mesmerized. My hair is long and flowing around my shoulders, and though it's a little rough, it is shiny and healthy looking. Remnants of a smile still linger and I notice that my cheeks are slightly flushed, but only vaguely through the transparency of the window. I can barely see my scar, lightened and veiled in the clear glass.

Leon's face appears in the glass behind me. He must have wanted to see what I am staring at and I am aware that he is staring intensely at my reflection too. But not intense in the way that Gramma had, but in another way entirely. Suddenly, I turn around and catch him in the act. My movement surprises him and he turns away too late.

"Sorry," I hear him mumble quietly.

We both step out into the hall. It is not as busy as it was the last time and we take up a quickened but easy pace. Leon takes the lead early and I step behind him, following him down what seems to be an impossible maze of white walls and mysterious doors.

As we turn down another wide hallway, we are met by shrieks. A young girl, possibly my age, perhaps younger, is screaming and thrashing around in a wheelchair. The sound is shrill and terrible and I close my eyes and put my hands over my ears, but I cannot stop a terrifying vision from erupting into my conscious.

Screaming.

The sound floods my ears and flashing bright lights pop in front of my eyes. But then it leaves as quickly as it comes. I open my eyes and Leon's face is right in front of mine. His eyes are startled with concern and something else; it might have been sadness. I close my eyes again and try to steady myself. I take a deep breath and let the world right itself in front of me. I remember how easy it is to shatter this precious place, and how I have to be so careful to not let it slip from my grasp.

"Don't be afraid, Katerina. You're okay." Leon's words come soft and swift, words that hold me here, moment by moment. When I open my eyes again, I see that the screaming girl has been wheeled away and now there is no one but Leon and I standing in the hallway. "We're almost to the activity room," Leon encourages and adds, "But we need to hurry. I'm supposed to make sure that you arrive on time."

I nod and we start walking again, finally approaching a door decorated with paper snowflakes and brightly colored construction paper. One of the pieces of paper has my name with a headshot photo on it taped next to pictures of other people. I reach up to touch my picture; I'm not smiling in it, but someone's drawn smiley faces and stars beside it so that I might seem more cheerful. Leon twists the handle and opens the door.

"I've got a delivery for you, Sanjay," Leon says merrily, entering the room and pulling me in behind him.

"Oh, good morning, Leon!" the man called Sanjay answers; he is faced away from us, sitting on a chair. I look around. The room is wide with butter yellow walls and there are twelve folding chairs including Sanjay's in a circle. A few people are sitting in some of the chairs, some are talking to each other energetically, but a few are keeping to themselves, looking down or at the wall.

"Katerina!" Sanjay exclaims, rising to greet me at the door. "It's so wonderful to have you joining us again. Mrs. Babbitt tells me that you have made quite a recovery. How excellent!"

His warm greeting surprises me, but already I am starting to like Sanjay. From his warm olive colored skin and comforting brown eyes, his presence is immediately calming and likable. His long dark hair is pulled back in a loose ponytail and square black-rimmed glasses are perched on his nose. He doesn't look too much older than Leon or I, but he holds himself with the most knowing and sympathetic manner, which makes him seem much older.

"This is our trial run," Leon continues, "So I'll be waiting right outside if something happens."

"Thanks Leon. I'm sure that it means a lot to Katerina if you stay close by." Sanjay turns and smiles at me with the most genuinely warm smile. "Thank you for joining back with us today. We've missed you. I'm glad that you are feeling better." His words are so sincere and they make me feel so comforted and welcomed.

"Good luck," Leon says and starts to head outside the door. "I'll be right outside if you need me, okay?" I nod.

"Katerina, why don't you have a seat across from Charlotte?" Sanjay suggests and directs me to one of the open chairs in the circle. I turn my head to look at the person he is gesturing to and my heart stops. The ghost woman is staring at me. I am frozen and dare not move; I know that if I keep moving toward her, I will be torn painfully from this dream. I think about Leon and imagine his hand squeezing my arm gently.

You're okay, Katerina. You're okay. The ghost woman cannot take her eyes off of me and, in my mind, I know that the delicate threads that hold me here are unraveling rapidly.

"Katerina," Sanjay's soothing voice touches my consciousness, "Are you alright?"

I take a tentative step toward my chair and the world remains still. I step again, each one more cautious than the next. I let out a deep breath as I make it to my chair and sit down. I look over at the ghost woman. *What is she doing here?* This is *my* dream, *my* escape. She has no right to be here, infecting it with the realities of the waking world.

"I'd like to take a minute to welcome everyone to today's session. And I'd like to take the opportunity to welcome back a very special person to our group today, Katerina. We are so glad to have you back with us today."

He claps his hands together and a few people around the circle join him. I don't look at him; my eyes are fixated on the ghost woman. I wish she would just disappear entirely before she gives us both away, bringing in the reality that has no place here.

"So Katerina," Sanjay begins and I jerk my eyes over to see his face. Immediately, I feel at ease. "How do you feel today?"

Everyone seems to want to know how I feel today, and truthfully, except for a few things, like the ghost woman and the screaming girl in the hall, I have never felt better. It is one of the first times in recent months that I have not felt like I am trying to escape from something. Sanjay's face is so kind and concerned that it makes me want to be honest. I am not used to people being concerned about my well-being.

"Fine," I answer him. The ghost woman is here, but I keep my ground. I'm not fading. I am here. The world isn't splitting apart, but I can't shake the feeling that something still isn't right, that something is missing.

"Leon tells me that you've been out to the courtyard," Sanjay states, interrupting my thoughts. "How did you like it?"

The courtyard. Out under the sun. My heart wells just remembering it, with its lush greenery and inherent tranquility. "It was wonderful. I hope that I might go back to it soon."

Sanjay looks at me with a most interested look, like something in my answer surprises him. He smiles approvingly, and then his face changes, like he is debating on asking me his next question. My mind is still lingering on the courtyard and I decide that when Allie and I leave our confinement, that no matter where we end up, I want to have a garden like that. I go to look at him, but look past him and notice there is a clock up on the wall. It's only been twenty minutes, but it feels like hours that I have been here, plagued by the ghost woman reminding me that this peaceful place is all too good to last. Sanjay doesn't ask me any more questions and I sit back, waiting for whatever this is to be over.

I let my mind drift back to Allie. But the image of her in my mind is fading. I had to get back to her. She needs me. She will be there when I wake up, waiting for me to execute our next set of plans. And as hard as it is to give up the sunlight, and the kind smiles, and the security of Leon's comforting presence, I will go back to her. Our plan has to work, we have to break free of Uncle's house. There is no other option. Through all the torment and the pain, I had promised hope for Allie. I have given her a dream for new possibilities in a life where she will no longer know the hell that we have lived in for so long.

But when I am here, Allie seems so distant, like more than a dream divides us. I cling to her with desperate fingers, but she slips like air between them. I am selfish and I know it; how can I ever be happy when she isn't here? The guilt is a torrent that courses through me. How can I feel anger toward the ghost woman for reminding me of my responsibilities? I should feel angry with myself for becoming so attached, so anchored into this place. This place that isn't even real. Sanjay is talking to the ghost woman again, and this time when I look into her faded eyes, I know we are not enemies. My mind feels like it is dancing on a bubble about ready to burst, but I am not ready for it.

"I have to go," I announce aloud, calmly but decidedly, keeping the bubble at bay.

"So soon?" Sanjay questions, the concern enveloping his face again. "Are you feeling okay? Do you need me to go get Mrs. Babbitt?"

"No," I reply, sounding more lucid, "I'm just a little tired. If it's okay with you, can I ask Leon to take me back to my room now?" It is just a little lie, but I know if I can get back to the bed, then Allie will not be too far away.

He seems surprised at my composed and articulate response, like he is expecting me to react in another way entirely. I don't collapse or fade at all.

Face still puzzled by my request, Sanjay nods. "Certainly Katerina, though you know you are more than welcome to stay." I nod, but the image of Allie in my mind is fading fast and I have the worst feeling that I might not be able to make it back to her.

Leon appears in the doorway, like he is on cue, and I walk over to him silently.

"Is everything alright?" he whispers, so as not to disturb the rest of the room. I nod again. He leads me out into the hallway and we start our walk back to my room.

"You didn't stay for very long," he comments.

"I know. I'm just a little tired." The world is not spinning, there are no threats to pull me from this place. My mind is a clear pool, shallow like glass on the top, but I will not allow myself to plunge deeper into the darkness below it.

Leon also seems surprised at me, but he does not say anything. He reaches for my arm, but I move away. He doesn't have to hold me here anymore. It is my choice now. Instead, I push myself onward. Back to Allie; she needs me, and I her.

Once back in the room, I lie down on the bed and shut my eyes. I don't even notice Leon's presence anymore, whether he stays or leaves. My world does not come back to me as quick as it

A Veil of Shattered Dreams

usually does and I squeeze my eyes even harder shut. I lie there for what seems like days, but finally the darkness that I used to shun carries me sweetly back to my sister.

Treasure

My eyes wrench open, and like resurfacing from a cavernous pool, I take a deep ragged breath. Darkness warps in front of my eyes. Reorienting myself is difficult because my head is heavy with sleep and it feels as though all my insides are scrambled.

Allie. The one singular thought echoes in the lonely caverns of my head. *Allie.* Frantic and desperate to hold her close to me, I strip back the covers expecting to see her tiny frame snuggled against mine. But she is nowhere to be seen. Where is she? Doesn't she know that I need her?

Rising from the bed, bare feet padding on the carpet, I stumble through the blackness out into the hall. Night cloaks everything, making it nearly impossible to see, except for the fuzzy outlines of the walls and the banister before me. I run my hands behind me along the wall, feeling gently as I creep for the doorway that will lead me to Allie. Tiptoeing carefully as not to wake the house, knowing how devastating that will be this time of night, I make my way into Allie's room.

The room is much smaller than mine. Her bed juts out and I almost trip over it in the dark.

"Allie," I call, slightly above a whisper. I hear her low deep breathing and my heart leaps slightly. As I kneel down beside her bed, her head turns towards me, but she is not awake. Even in the suppressive darkness, I can make out the peaceful curve of her mouth and the paleness of her cheeks. How soft she looks, how fragile. Gently, I lift my hand and brush a strand of wispy hair out her face and tuck it behind her ear.

I'm here. The vivid dreams with Leon seem only vague memories of light and color. And loss. I'm here with Allie and it's the only thing that matters. I slide carefully into the bed beside her and cuddle up next to her. "I'm here Allie, I'm here," I murmur tenderly into her ear, "I won't leave you again." I close my eyes, but I will myself not to sleep.

Minutes pass, maybe even hours, and I focus my mind on the future. On our escape plan. I run through each of the motions in my mind, making a mental list of the supplies we have and what we still need. Allie has grown quiet, her breathing not as pronounced. The silence makes me restless. I flip over on my back, but I cannot remain still. I realize that there is still so much that needs to be done before the next grocery day and our time is running out.

If I can be quiet enough, I think to myself, *I may be able to sneak down the stairs while it is still dark and quickly get some more supplies.* Rising slowly, as not to wake Allie, I make my way over to the door. Glancing back at her, I smile and then focus my mind on the task ahead.

First-aid, canned foods, Allie and mine's old sleeping bags, cash. I run through some of the list items in my head. The cash is going to be the difficult part. I am aiming for the change jar that Uncle keeps on top of the refrigerator. Every day when Uncle comes home from work, he empties any change that he carries in his pockets into the jar. What he uses the money for, I do not know, but it is never counted until the end of every other month. He will not know that I have taken anything until after I am long gone.

It's very dark and I move blindly and silently into the hallway, feeling my way along the wall until the outline of the banister comes into focus. Gripping it with two hands, I cautiously place one foot tentatively on the first step. The house is deadly still. I don't know what time it is or even how much time I have. Every minute sound, every little thing that I accidently knock into or bump slightly sounds exaggerated and deafening. Creeping down the steps, I try to calculate how long it will take me to gather everything, take it carefully back upstairs and hide it, all without waking up Uncle, or before he wakes up.

Reaching the bottom of the stairs, my hands feel the lightly raised texture on the wall of the hallway and I let it guide me towards my destination at the end of the hall, the coat closet. Reaching it, I grope my hand out for the closet door and my fingers smack into the knob.

Ping!

The tinny metal sound reverberates like a bell. My heart feels like it might collapse. I stop, holding my breath to listen for an inkling of any footstep or creaks of someone else moving about. Not hearing anything, I ease the door open and peer intently inside. But, inside the closet, the darkness is even more absolute than in the hallway. Slowly I reach up on the top shelf for

Allie and mine's sleeping bags. I scan the edge of the wood shelf with my fingertips, feeling around for the smooth polyester material. Exhilaration flows as my fingers encounter my target. Straining upward onto my tip toes, I can almost reach the cord that binds the roll together and I lurch myself with a small jump for it.

I miss.

Instead my hand knocks the sleeping bag and loosens it from its shelved position. It rolls out of my grasp and hits with a dull thump on the floor. I cannot believe it. Anger flushes through me. Why does everything have to go wrong? Why does the world have to conspire against *me*? I want to reach down and pummel the sleeping bag for almost ruining everything. In the back of my mind, time is becoming very conscious and I wonder how much of it I have already wasted. Lunging upward again, I managed to grasp the cord of the other sleeping bag and pull it into my arms without incident. Picking up the sleeping bag from the floor and hoisting it under my arm, I quickly shuffle out of the closet.

It isn't until I make it into the kitchen, shifting Allie and mine's sleeping bags in my arms, that I know that I haven't planned nearly well enough. I haven't thought of how I am going to reach the change jar. The cans of food are underneath the counter and are easy enough to roll up into the sleeping bags to muffle their sound. However, the jar is fragile and heavy with coins and one mistake will send it crashing down and shattering all over the floor. I grope for one of the kitchen chairs. It scrapes noisily across the floor, no matter how quietly or softly I pull it. Suddenly, the softest sound pierces the room. Freezing, I listen intently. It sounds like the padding of footsteps coming from above.

Hurriedly, I abandon the effort. Gathering the items that I have managed to grab, I dart up the stairs. Every nerve is tingling and the current coursing through me makes every hair stand on end. Any sudden movement will jolt me, spilling my contents down the steps. I anxiously scan the landing at the top of the stairs. It is empty. Whatever I thought was there had either gone back to bed or was something I had imagined. I dare not go back down the stairs; I probably won't be lucky with another false alarm.

Hiding the sleeping bags and the cans underneath my bed with the coats, I plop down on the covers. My breathing does not relax. I am tempted to go back to Allie's room, but I have already made enough noise; best not to risk it. My body is too on edge to sleep so I lie back, trying to calm myself, staring up at the ceiling until morning.

I find my mind drifting back to Leon. His face, his voice, his kindness, they won't leave me alone. I close my eyes and I see him smiling at me, the tendrils of my mind reach out to him and I feel the invisible hand on my shoulder again, but instead of it pulling me away, it pushes me toward Leon.

I'm not afraid to go there, to go to him, now that I know I can bring myself back. But I do not sleep. I do not dream. I only lie there, my heart being tugged in two different directions. How can I feel so right, so *real* there? How can a dream hold you and wrap you so completely inside of it that you ignore your obligations and responsibilities? How can it reach out and touch your soul and then throw reality in your face? Allie isn't there. She's here and no matter how far away I go, somehow she draws me back to her. I prepare for the onslaught of guilt I know that will punish me for this kind of thinking, but it does not come. The delicate threads in my mind aren't unraveling, but rather they are dancing and jerking me like a puppet on the end of them.

I don't sleep and suddenly the sun is rising and the light filters through the window, blinding me of all my thoughts. Blindness is bliss, to not have to think or feel. For a moment, I just want to *be*. And then, the moment passes in a deep breath and I rise to my feet so I can go wake Allie up for breakfast.

As we settle into our chairs at the breakfast table and begin to eat, Uncle eyes us suspiciously. "Can anyone tell me why in the hell when I got up this morning, my chair had been moved around and the coat closet door was wide open?" Uncle's voice penetrates the silence at the breakfast table. He knows. I avert my eyes from him, cursing myself furiously on the inside. Another mistake. How could I have forgotten? How could I have been so careless? Allie and I are going to have to pay for it.

"And since all the doors and windows are still locked and not broken, I'm sure no thieving bastards broke into the house and were looking in our coat closet in the middle of the night."

"I don't feel like I ask much of you," he continues in a mock dramatic show of hurt feelings, "but I keep a roof over your heads, I took you in. I've given you everything!" He rises from his chair, looking from me to Allie and back to me. "All of this, this damn sneaking around, scheming behind my back … IT WILL STOP!" He is shouting now, livid. Suddenly, Uncle takes both of us firmly by the arm and forces us up from the table.

"Where are we going?" Allie cries as Uncle half drags us away from the kitchen. He doesn't say a word, but continues to walk us down the hallway. The path is horribly familiar and it isn't until Uncle stops in front of a peeling old door, do I realize where he is taking us. Allie lets out an audible gasp, but he ignores her.

A year ago, I was first introduced to the Warehouse. Where most people have basements and cellars in their homes, we have the Warehouse. It is an unfinished place that lurks below the house where soil creeps in through the foundation, where various odds and ends, mostly junk and trash, have accumulated over the years. It is a desolate and decrepit place, where hulking spiders with their bulging backs hide, where black snakes weave their nests, and where the occasional larger beasts burrow into its dark damp depths. Even in the daytime, the Warehouse is pitch black, more of a cave than a crawlspace. Just imagining it raises the hairs on my skin and gives me goose bumps. Allie, realizing where we are going, is fearfully squirming around, trying to free herself from Uncle's grasp.

Last year, she accidentally fell down into the Warehouse. I searched the house for her, but I couldn't find her for hours. She eventually found her way back to the steps, but she didn't sleep without nightmares for days.

"Stop your sniffling," Uncle snaps at Allie. *It's okay*, I mouth to her, but the look on her face steals the air from my lungs. She is absolutely terrified. I will not let the fear touch me; I already realize that there are other things that I am more fearful of. Like losing Allie. Like being captive in a place with no chance of escape. This, the Warehouse, is only a battle of wills, a test of my devotion, my mental fortitude. I wish I can tell her that I am strong enough, that she has no reason to be afraid. But as I look into her eyes, all my thoughts disappear, and no mental preparation, no training, can prepare me for what I find there.

Complete surrender. She looks so different than what she has before, with those big open eyes.

It is a different fear she carries within her heart, a deeper one. It permeates her perfect features in ways I haven't cared to notice, in the shadows of her delicate face, in the boyish curve of her form. It goes farther than I am able to comprehend, and she looks at me with mingling fear that speaks to me in phrases I dare not interpret.

There it is again, that feeling of being pulled away, a stiff invisible hand on my shoulder trying to lead me away from here, from her. I push back at the invisible hand, concentrating only on Allie's face. The guilt is building again; no matter where I am, it will not leave me alone. It rubs against my heart until it is raw, and there is nothing that I can do about it.

As soon as Uncle opens the door, the wet decaying smell penetrates everything. This must be what death smells like. The dampness clings to the air like a cape of rotting flesh with darkness so tangible that it might reach out and devour us whole. Allie is whimpering again as soon as he shoves us onto the cold cement steps.

"I want all this debris gone through," he orders, looking more at me than Allie, "Everything that can be taken outside and burned, make a pile here." He gestures at the top of the steps. "Everything else stack near the bottom of the steps... And don't half-ass it. Or you can spend the whole day down here doing it the right way. Your choice," he states and slams the door on us and the darkness is all.

"Stay on the steps Allie," I say softly, trying to sound positive as the shadows engulf us. Every nerve is set on edge as a chill sweeps through my body. I close my eyes and just listen. Sometimes I've noticed that in the deep dark, if I'm quiet long enough, I can hear everything. Like Allie's soft quivering breath that lets me know how frightened she is and the whispering skitters of God knows what dragging its fat belly across the earthen floor. Suddenly, the door bursts open and the light that falls upon us is blessedly blinding. It cuts through the abyss and for half a second, I hope that he might have a change of heart.

"Yes, light is a wonderful thing, isn't it?" he says to us nastily and then tosses something to me. A flashlight. "Remember that I can give as well as take away. Say thank you Uncle." I hesitate, but his gaze fixes on me expectantly.

"Thank you Uncle," I manage to utter, not wanting him to hear the despair in my voice. The door slams shut again, and though it is not locked,

I don't dare to open it in case he is watching. I click on the flashlight and its little beam shoots through the black. It ignites the shadows and I whirl its dim ray around the stairs, the darkness fleeing before it. I shine it down onto the rest of the steps and try not to think about how much the damp cement and warped handrails that make up the stairwell remind me of the pictures of crypts that I've seen.

"It's alright Allie, see?" I take a step down. She sits on the first step with her arms wrapped around her knees and tearstains on her cheeks.

"I'm going to take the flashlight with me, okay?" I tell her and take another step down the staircase, a little bit into the dark. "You'll be okay, Allie. See that little sliver right there between the door and the floor? It'll help you not to be afraid." She looks behind her to the little light from the hallway peeking beneath the door. With the flashlight in front of me, I begin descending down into the Warehouse.

Uncle's house is relatively small with small windows and small doorways, which is why I am so surprised at how big the Warehouse is. There is quite a bit of empty space, but it is shrouded with thick cobwebs that hang like sheets from the ceiling. I can't help but think that they are perfectly human size, ready to trap the next prey. I have nothing but the flashlight, so I use my arm to bat the webs down. The sticky trap covers my arm and the side of my body, and I shake frantically, trying to knock the web off. The light from the flashlight bounces everywhere and I hear Allie call for me from the top of the steps.

"I'm alright!" I yell back to her, and I shine the flashlight around to see if I can see from one wall to the other. But the darkness and the webbing are thick and it is easy to see how one could get lost. A cold chill wracks my body as I try not to think of all the tiny spiders that might be crawling on me from the web. Piles and piles of garbage grow from the floor like stalagmites. Rotting cardboard and broken pieces of plastic bins mixed with ripped up paper juts out from the pile. Long forgotten belongings twist themselves around it like crude sculptures. The spires teeter precariously as the beam of the flashlight falls on them.

I take a cautious last few steps downward. Mortar and crumbling brick from the house supports are scattered like ruins, the smell of decay growing stronger with every step. The floor is surprisingly solid and I scan the area around me to be sure that nothing is lurking there. But the radius of my vision is small and the glow of the flashlight seems a bit dimmer. Slowly, I approach the first spire. There are so many things to pick from and I try to be careful not to pick the wrong thing, lest the whole mountain comes crashing down on me.

Mustering up as much courage as I can, I plunge my hand into the pile. Terror builds inside of me; I turn my head away from the junk.

"Kitty!" Allie cries and even though I am thoroughly freaked out, I remember that I must be brave for her. I don't even think before I tear back through the debris to the steps.

"I'm here Allie," I say breathlessly, trying to sound comforting, but then something catches my attention. Crawling on the wall right behind Allie is the biggest spider I have ever seen. My breath catches as I watch each of its eight long legs scuttling slowly on the stones behind her. Even from a distance, I can make out its form, its back, bulging and pulsing brown. It is only inches from her and I know how aggressive these can be.

"Allie," I say, trying to be calm, "Don't move." The spider moves quickly down the wall and onto the step she is sitting on. Allie's face follows where my eyes are looking. Her eyes widen and she raises her hand to shield herself as the spider crawls right over to her.

"Kitty!" Allie squeals and it's all the encouragement I need to race to the top of the stairs and bring my tennis shoe down on top of its spindly body. Fresh tears spill out over Allie's face and she wraps her arms around my knees. "I wanna go back in the house!" she sobs. My heart breaks seeing her so frightened.

"Maybe if you go and ask Uncle, he will let you go to the bathroom," I suggest. As soon as the words leave my mouth, Allie releases me and disappears behind the door.

After she leaves, I resume my task back down in the crypt. Two piles are steadily growing when I notice that the flashlight is not as bright as it had been. But I pay it no mind and use that as motivation in my effort. I continue to cautiously sort through the mounds of garbage that sprawl out before me.

Minutes pass, maybe an hour, I am not sure, but I am beginning to see a path marking the work I have done. I work carefully but relentlessly, fear skittering constantly down my spine, killing at least three more spiders that wander into my midst. I am in the middle of piecing through a rather large heap of trash when I am shrouded in absolute blackness.

The flashlight. Of course. It *would* run out of juice right when I am about halfway to the other side of the Warehouse. Cursing the flashlight into the fiery pit of Hades, I call out, wondering if my sister has come back.

"Allie!" I shout, but no one answers me. "ALLISON!" Silence. Wading blindly back through the mess and onto the path I have cleared, I start heading back to what I hope is the stairs. Trudging blindly up the steps, I know that the battle is only half done. Exiting into the hall, I make it only a few feet before Allie comes running up to me holding a messy peanut butter and jelly sandwich.

"Lunch?" Allie offers innocently, handing the sandwich off to me. Wiping my hands on my pants, I take it from her and eat a few bites as I walk toward the kitchen and peek inside. Uncle is sitting in his chair at the kitchen table eating his own lunch.

"Uncle," I say and he jerks his head nastily at me.

"I know you're not done," he snaps.

"Your flashlight died," I interject.

"So?"

"I need to see and I can't finish what you ask me to do unless I have new batteries." He looks at me as if he wants to say something, but pushes his chair out violently. Walking over to one of the cabinets, he pulls fresh batteries from the drawer, slamming it shut.

"Thank you, Uncle," I say as sincerely as possible. I can play his game. Just have to keep him pacified until grocery day, just a few more days.

"Go," he barks. I realize why I endure this long, because it is all quickly coming to an end. Not waiting until he turns back around, I hurry back to the Warehouse door, cramming the last bites of peanut butter and jelly sandwich into my mouth. Wiping the crumbs off on my pants, I exchange the dead batteries for the new ones. Allie reluctantly follows me to the door. She looks better, calmer. I take a hold of her hand and lead her back into the dark.

"Stay right here," I tell Allie and I descend back into the pit, turning the flashlight back on.

Back in the abyss, I walk slowly through the path I have made through the towering piles of junk.

As I shine the flashlight deeper into the dark, I notice a ratty knapsack on top of one of the spires. I reach for it, take it down off the pile, and inspect it. We can put some of our supplies in this. Shaking it out, I take it over to Allie and pronounce excitedly, "Look what I found! We can put some of our stuff in it, you know, for when we leave. Here, let's make another pile in case I find anything else useful." Allie takes the knapsack in her trembling hands. Running her tiny hands over it, she looks up at me with her tearstained face, eyes daring to hope a little. I rub her shoulder reassuringly and she clings to the bag, knotting her fingers in it.

The discovery of the knapsack releases a torrent inside of me. The dreaded pit has become the treasure trove. What has been one of Allie's greatest fears might become one of our greatest allies. I attack the next few spires with intensity, sifting through all the contents carefully, pulling out the items that Uncle has asked, but also stashing some of them with Allie at the steps. After each time I take something back to Allie, I journey further into the dark. Just as it feels like the darkness might swallow me, I brandish the flashlight ahead, keeping myself on the path. The adrenaline pulses through me with every step, with every treasure that I find for us to take. The thought occurs to me that we might actually make it out of here, that one of my plans might actually work out for us.

Venturing upstairs for a quick bathroom break, I hear the front door slam, signifying that Uncle has left the house because the ghost woman would never dare slam the door. I collect Allie and our supplies from the stairs. The Warehouse doesn't look like the same place. Pride floods through me, looking down on what I have accomplished. Once back in my room, we spread all of our loot out in front of us: two knapsacks, another blanket, one of the ghost woman's old wallets, a water bottle, and a plastic bag full of brand new unworn socks. We pack as much of the items as we can into one of the knapsacks, and pack our canned food in the other.

"Two more days," Allie whispers, "and then we can go find Daddy."

"Two more days," I agree and my nerves tingle a little, but I push them away quickly. "You remember what you have to do?" Allie nods. "But instead of just taking the keys, I want you to take her wallet too, okay? We'll need as much cash as we can get if we're going to get away from here." Allie nods again, but when she looks up, her mouth turns into a giggle.

"Gramma will be so mad."

"Yes she will, but we should be long gone by the time she comes looking for us."

"Are you afraid that we're going to get caught again?" Allie questions, her little eyes darting to the door and then back to me.

"No," I say truthfully. "It's going to work this time."

The truth is, I don't know what the consequences will be, but we can't afford to think like that. Hopefully we will never have to face the consequences.

After hiding the rest of our supplies, I stretch out onto my bed and close my eyes. Allie climbs on the bed and curls up beside me. Having her next to me is all. Everything I risk is worth it for her. I cannot fail her again. I just can't. Closing my eyes, sleep takes me immediately.

Scrabble

My eyes open and I stare up to what I now know is not my bedroom ceiling. As my consciousness builds, it feels as though an invisible weight has been placed upon my chest. There is a daunting feeling that encircles my thoughts, like I might not be able to return home for a while. Allie was just right here; I had felt her breath and her body, assurance that I would never leave her again. *Why was it not enough to keep me with her?* I close my eyes again and picture her sleeping form at peace by my side. As I lay here, I will myself to try and wake up, but my brain will not rest. It is active and ahead of the rest of my being. Eagerly, my body and senses acclimate back to this place, leaving my mind fighting, using all of my concentration to return to Allie.

"Katerina, are you awake?" Leon's familiar voice shatters my focus. My mind loses the battle instantly and Allie's face is gone. My senses take over, choosing for me to be here. Slowly, I rise up to sit with my hands rubbing my bleary eyes. Leon is standing in the doorway, his hands on either side of the frame.

"Well, I'm not sure," I reply with a grin and then ask, "Why are you always here?"

"Mrs. Babbitt usually asks me to come check on you in the morning," Leon answers, trying to be nonchalant. He seems unusually distant and it perturbs me a little.

"Did she ask you to check on me today?" I question, curiosity growing.

"No," he says hesitantly, "I mean, Mrs. Babbitt's not here today." He quickly averts his gaze from me, his voice faltering, "I mean, I can always leave, if you want." He backs a little way out of the frame and into the hall.

"No," I respond quickly, "please stay." He looks relieved at my words and walks inside the room. "Come sit with me," I offer and point to the plain mint green armchair sitting in the corner of the room. Leon drags the armchair, scraping it across the floor, over beside the bed and plops down in it.

A Veil of Shattered Dreams

"So what do you have for me to do today?" The words come out more enthusiastic than what I really mean for them. But if I am going to have to be here, then I have decided that I might as well make the best of it. Maybe I have started coming to terms with sharing myself between two worlds.

"No idea," he says, looking at me and laughing softly. "What do you *want* to do today?" He sounds as if his voice has a little melancholy in it and then I remember that it always sounds a little sad, but I have never once wondered why.

"I'd like to do something fun," I reply.

"Well, we can always go to the rec room."

"What's in the rec room?"

"You know, a pool table, board games, stuff like that."

"Do you think they have Scrabble?"

"I'm pretty sure they do."

"My dad and I used to play Scrabble together," and I'm struck by the face of my dad. It stuns me how quickly the memory erupts into my consciousness.

"K-A-T, Kat," Dad says stacking the tiles on the game board.

"Daaad!"

"What?" he asks, grinning.

"That's not how you spell cat!"

"That's how I spell my Kitty-Kat." Smiling from ear to ear, I move his tiles off the board.

"Okay, hug time for my smart girl," Dad says and reaches out for me and wraps his arms around me. *"You're my girl, aren't cha?"* I nod ferociously in his arms, leaning against his chest.

"Well since I can't make any more words," he taps my nose affectionately, *"I guess you win."* Giggling, I reach for the score pad and begin to check our scores.

"I do win," I supply, smiling again.

"Ahh, you're getting too good at this game."

The flashback leaves as quickly as it came. I miss him so much. I will never understand how he could just leave us the way he did. Allie, as young as she is, was easily forgiving, but I'm not.

Leon touches me gently on the shoulder and it pulls me out of my thoughts.

"You ready?" he asks, but I know that it is the equivalent of *"Are you okay?"*

"Yeah," I answer both questions, rising from the bed.

Leon is already up and heading to the door. Going to meet him, I slide my bare feet into a pair of sensible brown slippers and pull on the thin robe that was draped on the edge of the bed. As we exit into the hall, he shuts the room door behind us. Walking along, a nervous excitement is building up inside of me like the first time. Leon leads me down a series of hallways to a door that is very different from any of the others I've seen. This door is painted a shocking shade of bright blue and I can't help but feel cheerful just looking at it.

This place, I decide, is full of surprises. Leon is smiling again; I guess the door makes him feel happy too. In this moment, I'm having a hard time remembering why I wanted to leave here. But then I realize that this is the first time I have felt happy in a very long time, that the guilt hasn't immediately surfaced and tried to drag me away. Even when the word 'guilt' crosses my mind, I wait to see if the corresponding emotion will come, as if I can summon it with my thoughts.

Pausing, I place my hand on the bright door and wait, but it doesn't come. I try to think of Allie, the guilt trigger, but instead of finding her smiling face, I find hope. I'm not worried about getting back to her for once. I know that I will go back to her eventually. She will be there when I return and I will keep my promise to her. But the urgency is gone. I push the blue door open and take in the room that appears before me.

There are people here. My nerves pulse, the tiniest bit on edge. Before I can change my mind about being here, one man with scrawling tattoos on both of his forearms booms loudly, "Good mornin' Leon! I was beginning to wonder if you'd ever bring her here!" The man is bent over an old pool table, green felt peeling and wood marred. It seems he was about to take a shot when we walked in.

I shoot Leon a quizzical look, but he ignores me and defends to the man, "Mrs. Babbitt gives me strict orders; she doesn't want Katerina to overdo it."

"Oh, you know how Louise is, I don't know about that woman sometimes. Her and her damn meds. You know what I think; they've forgotten how to treat people. Just dope 'em up and leave 'em. But I tell you Leon, I been on the dope. I've been on just about everything under the sun, but nothing makes it better. People, Leon, that's the ticket, people make it better," the burly man rants.

His opponents are a set of androgynous twins. They're almost completely identical, even in their movements. Watching them is mesmerizing, like a wave break - one is the crest and one the trough.

The tattooed man lays down his pool stick and starts walking towards us. "Well, don't be rude Leon," the man chastises good-naturedly. But before Leon has a chance to react, the man stops in front of me. His face is very pleasant and awfully familiar.

"She's not going to remem…" Leon starts, but the man cuts him off with a dismissive wave of his hand.

"Pardon my friend Leon, lovely lady," he speaks directly to me, "it seems as though he has forgotten his manners." He takes my hand and shakes it warmly. "I'm Randy, and this is Penny and Petey." He gestures to his pool opponents. Something stirs within me, a nagging, but an impossible to sate feeling that is right on the brink of realization. They don't say anything, looking at me with double intense stares.

"It's alright y'all, she's a friend of Leon's." The twins continue to stare warily at me.

"I'm Katerina," I introduce softly, giving them a half-smile.

Sauntering back over to the pool table, Randy picks up the cue stick and invites me to join him,

"Well then, Miss Katerina, why don't you come on over here and let ole Randy show you a thing or two about the time honored game of billiards." I glance at Leon and see him nod encouragingly, so I step up beside the tattooed man.

"Thatta girl, now, take the cue stick here and place it long ways with the tip between your pointer and middle finger," Randy instructs, demonstrating. I nod. He hands the stick off to me and helps me line up for what I see as a not too difficult shot into a corner pocket.

I lengthen my body and lean over the table, listening to Randy's careful instructions. I draw back my arm, lining the stick point up with the pool balls on the table. In a quick moment, I get ready to make my shot and I almost feel an invisible arm tugging on my shoulder.

"Now Kitty Kat, remember how I told you to line up that shot. Keep your arm relaxed. Don't think too much about it. Just picture your cue making contact with the ball. Pull your arm back, take a deep breath, and then release."

And Dad is here; I can almost see him, almost feel him standing right next to me. A rivet of lightning excitement licks through my body and makes me lose my concentration and my arm slips, the stick wobbling in my grasp. Unnaturally astute, Randy notices my slipup and looks from me to my audience. His mouth splits open in a devilish grin.

"It's all right darlin', try again," Randy heartens and helps me straighten up my cue stick. Pulling my arm back again for the shot, I release. With a smacking crack, the stick hits the cue ball, sinking the first ball into the recesses of the corner pocket. A spurt of joy courses through me. Never before have I felt so proud or capable of anything in my entire life.

"You're a natural!" Randy exclaims, and in that moment I almost forget that I'm the girl who's even best laid plans went to hell. I don't even know that girl who wallowed in the guilt of letting people down. I am ecstatic. The twins glance over toward me, identical looks of approval visible on their faces.

It is only one shot, but I feel as if it is my whole world. Randy claps me on the shoulder warmly, "Welcome to the crew Katerina! You should come and hang out with us more often." I hand the cue stick back to Randy, who turns his attention back to the pool table and begins intently deciphering the twins' available moves.

"Great job, hotshot," Leon walks over to the pool table and winks at me. "Look what I've got." He waves a maroon colored box in front of my face. I positively beam as the light fills my eyes.

"So do you want to play?"

"Well I have to warn you, I'm a lot better at Scrabble than I am at pool," I admit.

"I'll take that challenge," Leon contests.

"Have fun you two," Randy says, then focuses his attention back on the twins, "Okay you both, you're going down now."

Leon leads me over to a corner where two squashy armchairs sit with a little wooden table resting in the middle between them. Sitting down in one of the chairs, he lays the game board and tiles out on the table.

"My dad used to play Scrabble with me when I was a little girl," I share casually.

"Really?" Leon asks interestedly.

"Yeah, he used to let me win, but then I started actually getting pretty good... but," I sigh, "that was a long time ago."

"It sounds like you were pretty close to him."

"Yeah, we were," I agree, but as I dwell on the words, I feel the subtle tears well in my heart. "Then he left me."

A Veil of Shattered Dreams

I miss my dad so much. And as much as I try to not let my anger and resentment toward him mar the much happier memories, it takes all that I have from keeping those bitter emotions from spilling over. Leon dumps himself a pile of letters and shakes the tile bag, offering it to me.

"So what about you? I feel like I talk about *myself* all the time. You never say anything about *yourself*," I query. Leon's eyes perk at my question, but he hesitates in answering. "Come on now, what about your dad?" I urge.

Leon lets out a deep heavy sigh, "Nothing to tell really. I didn't know him." The conversation went from lighthearted to very serious, very fast.

"Oh," I say gently, feeling like I might have brought up an uncomfortable subject.

"It's okay. I don't mind telling people. It's just a part of who I am. I don't know him because I don't care to know who he is."

He shrugs the admission off, but I can see in his eyes that his thoughts are still lingering on it.

"You're a good person, Leon," I say, trying to lighten the mood. "I can't tell you how much you being here means to me," I say sincerely. And it did mean a lot to me. My heart pangs in my chest and a realization strikes me so painfully.

None of this feels real to me. I reach out and scoop a handful of Scrabble tiles in my palm and feel the smooth wood of the pieces, worn from years of use. They feel real, every single tangible tile is part of a zinging awareness. I look up and into Leon's face, into his lovely blue eyes and warm dark skin. He leans across the table toward me and I can make out every facet of his features. The creases in his forehead are full of secrets and days of his life that I know not of. His impression in my mind is too great. I know that I will not be able to forget him. I want to stay here, I decide, in this dream that is too real to be a dream, but too strange and too different to be reality.

"Katerina," Leon's voice interrupts my thoughts, "It's your turn." I look at the game board to the word Leon has placed. Spilling out the handful of tiles in front of me, I skim through them to make an appropriate move. "So you never told me," Leon continues, "how you got that scar on your eyebrow." My hand reaches up instinctively and caresses the raised scar.

"It was an accident, I don't really know..." Where had the scar come from again? *That's right*, I remember, *from the kitchen cabinet*. That time Uncle came up from behind me unexpectedly, startling me and causing me to scrape myself on the corner of the cabinet door.

Or was it? Like a glimmering facet, or a thin fabric fluttering in a light breeze, a little pulse point begins to grow in my thoughts. The scar. There is something more familiar about it, more recent. I press my fingers against it, shutting my eyes, trying to conjure up the memory. It won't come. Focusing my consciousness on the memory, I strain toward the pulse point, gently pull back the delicate cloth of the veil and brace myself to plunge into it.

Sounds of screaming seize and paralyze me. I can feel a great pressure pushing down on me and I can't breathe. There is loud squealing and a metallic crunch as I throw my hands up violently to protect my face. I taste blood. The screaming does not cease. Terror drives me out of the pulse point and my mind wrenches the veil back down, sealing out the pain. My dream and Leon whirl around me precariously before coming to standstill.

"Katerina!" Leon shouts. I look around. Scrabble tiles are plinking onto the floor in a cascade. I must have knocked them over when I shielded myself. Leon is at my side, his hand now firmly pressed into mine. Around the room, Randy and the twins are staring silently. "What happened? Tell me what happened?" Leon frantically asks, breaking his calm composure.

"Screaming…" I manage to gasp out. "Blood…" I shake my head, but my mind will not let me go back there.

"Hey, you're okay. Breathe," Leon reassures, "you're okay."

I gaze over at him; there is something different on his face. Surprise? Relief? There is a tone behind his eyes that sharpens his features, like something has been fulfilled in them. The pulse point is throbbing, threating to explode over my thoughts. I know that I will have to confront it again soon.

"You're getting closer, you're doing so well," Leon says like he can see what I am thinking. He leans down and begins picking the tiles up off the floor and rearranging them back on the board. "It's getting more and more bearable every day. I knew it would." I have no idea what Leon is talking about and his cryptic words sound more menacing than helpful. He straightens up and stands over me, staring at me intently.

"You're starting to remember! Your scar. Your sister, Allie," he exclaims, looking deep into my eyes expectantly.

"Remember what? How do you know about Allie?" I ask sharply and rise up to meet him. Leon's words catch me severely off guard and we stare at each other for a tense moment. This is the first time that Leon has ever made me feel ill at ease and the eagerness and change in his tone is almost frightening.

"Enough, Leon," Randy cuts in. "I think she's had enough for today. Talk about something else." Leon glances over at Randy and then back at me.

"You know that I only want to help you," Leon says, his tone dropping back down as he backs away from me. I nod. Taking his seat again, he continues, "But I don't want to push you if you're not ready." Once again, he's completely lost me.

"You know, I have no clue what you're talking about," I say, hoping that the confusion is apparent in my voice.

"I know," Leon replies, shaking his head, "but you will."

"How do you know about Allie?" I ask again. His earlier comment has really unsettled me.

"Hey, I thought you were supposed to be asking me questions about myself. You said it yourself, we talk about you all the time."

"Yes, but..." I protest, trying to make him explain himself.

"No buts," Leon interrupts and I can't help but laugh at how confused I am now. Back and forth, I am constantly pulled from the edge of this dream. Always stuck between this world, Allie, and the pulse point. I'm afraid that the thin fabric in my brain might tear to shreds. And there it is again, glaring at me from the jumbled letter pile in front of me. "D-R-E-A-M-S, dreams," I say, spreading the letters over the game board. "And look, a triple word score."

"You really are good at this game, aren't you?"

"Only a little." Time for me to switch the subject on him. I start to bring up the subject of Allie again, but the look on his face tells me that I will not be getting any more information out of him about her. So instead I ask, "What's your mom like?"

"*My* mom?" Leon asks in surprise. "She was the most beautiful woman in the world and the sweetest. She used to mail me postcards from wherever she went. She had this way with words that made you feel like you were there with her," he explains, spelling the word "drip" out onto the table with my "d."

"You didn't go with her?" I shuffle through my own letters searching for the right word.

"No," Leon answers solemnly. "My mother was sold into sex trafficking. And she was the mistress of one of the infamous drug lords in Colombia. They traveled all over the globe, jet setting from one place to the other, staying out of the public eye."

"You're kidding," I interject in disbelief, spelling "muster" down on the board.

"I swear I'm not," he continues. "For a time, they laid low in Africa, down in eastern Ghana. Where my mother met my father." *Ah, brown skin, blue eyes.* I watch those eyes gaze at the game board intently. So unique, just like he is.

"How did you end up in America?"

"Well, after the drug lord found out she was pregnant with me, he arranged an abortion in the States. But my mother refused and had me here. But she was forced to abandon me. She always kept in contact with me, secretly, until she died." I scoff at Leon's word "run" but it blocks the tile that I want to use.

"I'm sorry," I say, absorbing every incredible word. And I feel like I have a new appreciation for Leon and the fact that despite his trials, he still manages to emanate his gentle kindness.

"She was murdered by that drug lord," Leon says flatly, "and somehow I thought if I mixed myself up in drugs long enough, I would be able to find him."

"That's quite a story."

"It's true. Peoples' lives aren't always as simple as they seem." I nod. There is a lot of truth to his words. "Your dad loves you. And just like my mom, he didn't want to leave you. Things just happen that way sometimes."

"I don't know. I wish that was true."

"I used to tell myself that she would come back for me. It took me a long time to come to terms with it and accept that she was never going to come back." In the back of my mind, I watch a replay of a small red Chevy driving down an empty dirt road with no promise of return, stranding two small girls in a living nightmare. Suddenly, Leon looks down at the small digital watch on his wrist.

"Ah, it seems that time has gotten away from me," he sighs. "I've got to get you back to your room."

"But we're still playing," I protest.

"I know, but I don't make the rules. And I've bent them as much as Mrs. Babbitt will let me."

"I don't want to leave."

"Look, I will keep the game out, just like it is and we can come back and finish it another time." Considering his offer, I reluctantly nod in agreement, get up from the armchair, and move to the door.

"Y'all leaving us?" Randy calls from the other side of the room. He and the twins are now playing a video game in front of an old television set.

"Unfortunately," Leon says and rises, following behind me.

"Ah, okay. Well, Katerina you come back to us as soon as you can."

"I will," I promise and let Leon steer me out the door.

We make our way down the hallways to the room and Leon waits at the door as I remove my slippers and robe and climb into bed.

"Today was fun," I comment. "It's nice to actually have friends to spend time with." Leon smiles.

"Yes it was," he agrees. "Well I guess I will see you later."

"Oh," I exclaim, "you're leaving?"

"Yeah."

"Can't you just stay a little longer? I'd really like to hear another story." With another softer, kinder smile, Leon walks into the room and takes a seat in the armchair beside the bed.

"Sure, what do you want to know?"

"Anything."

"Well, I have a pet iguana."

"Really?"

"Yep. And I named him San Juan because at the store they told me that he was from Puerto Rico."

"You're silly."

"It's true!" and he continues on talking about San Juan in that calm and comforting voice that I know so well. It lulls me and relaxes me. Leon's face is the last thing I see before my eyes close and sleep takes me.

Trapped

"Allie?" I mumble, waking to the sound of movement in the darkness. The lights turn on in the room and even with my eyes closed, I realize Allie is not here.

"What did you say, Katerina dear?" a concerned female voice asks, sounding close to the bed.

Something is wrong. Very wrong. I dare not peek yet. Behind my eyelids, I pretend to not be aware of what is happening. It cannot be. My heart lurches forward in my chest and thumps loudly against my ribcage. I should have gone back. Why have I not awakened? I tighten my closed eyes firmly, hoping that when I finally open them, everything will right itself.

"Dinner time, and look - roast beef with mashed potatoes! Looks delicious! And well, what do you know, you're allowed a chocolate brownie!

What a treat!" the soft female voice chimes cheerfully and only solidifies my dread and fear.

Why am I still here? *"Wake up!"* I scream in my mind. *"Wake up! Allie needs you!"* Terror shoots through my veins as I feel myself becoming more and more aware.

"Katerina, time to wake up," the voice is impatient now, almost scolding. I let my eyes slide open slowly and the stern brown eyes of Mrs. Babbitt are staring directly into mine. Disbelief mingles with confusion at the persistence of this dream and I wonder fearfully what the cause may be. My eyes widen, drinking in this scene, and I am more afraid now than I have ever been.

"Is something wrong, hon?" Mrs. Babbitt inquires gently, setting a tray with food down in front of me. The smell of the meal wafts up into my nostrils, nauseatingly vivid, causing my stomach to churn. Turning my head away from the food, I glance around the room nervously.

"Where's Leon?" I ask, growing a little anxious when I see that he is nowhere in sight.

"Well, he can't stay here all the time," Mrs. Babbitt replies in a condescending tone that sounds like she is explaining something simple to a child. But as I digest her words, I realize how completely alone I feel. Darkness has fallen outside the usually bright window. The whole room is almost unrecognizable, like an alien landscape bathed in lamplight and shadow. Suddenly I'm very aware of this darkness, that it isn't the darkness of my mind, but something very real.

"Don't worry, you'll see him soon enough. Now go ahead and eat your dinner. Oh, and let's not forget our meds," she continues bubbly, popping the lid off an orange pill bottle and dumping a few large pills into a plastic cup. Placing the plastic cup onto the food tray, she looks at me expectantly. Shaking my head, I look up at her uncertainly. Noticing the expression on my face, Mrs. Babbitt does something I never expected of her; she sits down on the edge of the bed. Sighing, she looks down at her hands in her lap.

"Katerina, you've got to eat something, sweetie," she speaks quietly, pausing to look up at me. I just stare at her blank-faced. This is punishment, I realize now. This is my mind punishing me for enjoying my time away from Allie. The dream earlier today had been so wonderful and I remember that I had wanted to stay. And now here I am, lying in this uncomfortable metal contraption of a bed, without Leon and without Allie.

My brain feels as if it is warring against itself and my own desires and dreams are the casualties of guilt and loneliness. The pulse point throbs vicious and unforgiving, lashing out angrily at my vulnerable mind. I feel it provoking me, taunting me with the secrets and memories it possesses. Tonight it seems there is no solace, there is no hope of making it back to Allie. And there is a gnawing sorrow that mixes in with everything, horribly familiar and ever growing in the tangle of thoughts and fragments holding steady at the battle lines.

As if my body is acting upon its own accord, my hand reaches out for a fork, scooping a blob of mashed potatoes off the dish and into my mouth. Mrs. Babbitt smiles gently and slides a glass of water and the cup of pills toward me on the tray.

"Go ahead and take your meds and I promise that I won't bother you anymore tonight," Mrs. Babbitt bargains and I can't help but sigh to myself. She thinks *she* is the one causing my problems. If she only knew. It's not her, it's me. And I'm so frustrated with myself and my predicament. Just wanting to be left with my thoughts, I reach out and grasp the cup of pills and dump them with a swig of water down my throat.

"See, that wasn't so bad," Mrs. Babbitt soothes as she stands. "Well, finish your dinner Katerina, and I'll check on you later." Heading for the door, she turns around to look over me one last time, and then exits.

Picking up my fork, I look at the food in front of me, but I have no appetite. All I care about is finding my way home, back to Allie. Back to where we would be leaving soon, our plans made, for a new and better life. If only I could *get* back. How could I have gotten so tangled up and twisted around, like a thick fabric had woven inside my mind, impenetrable and so complete? Sliding a little gob of mashed potatoes around, I break the potato mound and watch the river of gravy flow down over my plate, flooding the rest of the food.

If only Leon was here, he would help me get back, or at least help me to understand why I am still here. But even Leon is gone, and I don't understand why he would leave me at a time like this. A time that I need him the most. If this is all a dream, then why would my mind pull him away now? *Leon!* I call in my head, and hope that wherever he is in my subconscious, that he knows how much I need him now. I wait a few seconds, hoping that my mental summons might receive a reply.

Nothing. Everything is quiet. Too quiet. The absence of the usual noises of the hallway seems even more peculiar to me. But my thoughts, they are loud with questions and demands, wanting me to find a way back home, tempting me with swirling pinpricks of darkness and memories. I reach out to one of the memories, a tiny pearl glowing in the darkness. Desperate to escape from this place, I dive into the memory as it unfolds in a burst of light and color.

I bolt upright in my bed, surrounded by bright pink fluffy blankets, clutching a brown and tan stuffed cat, sobbing uncontrollably. The bedroom door bursts open and Dad rushes in, turning on the light.

"What is it Kitty Kat? What happened sweetheart?" he asks frantically, coming over to sit beside me on the bed.

A Veil of Shattered Dreams

"I-I had a bad dream Daddy! I was so s-s-scared!" The tears continue to fall as Dad gathers me into a big bear hug.

"You're okay Katerina, you're okay. I'm here," he says, still holding me close. "You don't ever have to be afraid because I'm right here." I cling to him tightly as he lays me back down in my bed and pulls a blanket over me.

"Nightmares don't last forever, it's over now." He sweeps a few stray hairs out of my face and kisses me on the forehead. I reach up for him, but he is fading.

The edges of the memory are blurring and I try to hold on to it longer. "Dad? Daddy come back, I'm scared!" I call out, and I clench my eyes closed trying to keep the memory from receding, but it dissipates quickly behind the veil and out of my reach.

A single tear slides out from the corner of one my closed eyes. I had forgotten that I still had that memory. I lift the tray of food off of my bed and put it on the stand next to me. Closing my eyes, I can't stop a flow of silent tears from trickling down my face. I lie back, watching the glimmering fragments of memories dancing behind my eyelids. The sadness, the darkness, and the memories whip around like a hurricane inside of my head. The veil is flapping wildly, threatening to tear. The battle is raging inside of my mind, but I am wounded and weary of fighting. And then suddenly, I'm not anywhere at all.

Shattered

I awake violently, gasping and sputtering. Gulping mouthfuls of air. My lungs are heavy and thick with the dampness of my room.

I'm back.

A wracking sob erupts over my senses and sends chills over my entire body.

I'm back.

My forehead is soaked with sweat. I push my damp messy hair away from my face with shaking hands. Climbing out of the bed gingerly, I move slowly because my reflexes are dulled by hours of deep sleep. Taking a few small steps, I try to steady myself, but then the gravity of everything, where I've been, the inner burden of my mind, weighs me down. I close my eyes and a wave of spiraling nausea sends me to my knees. Waiting for it to pass, I try to regain my footing, but the world is swaying and I am seconds from collapsing onto the carpet.

"Kitty? Are you awake?" a small voice cuts through my queasiness.

Allie. I can barely see her small form tiptoeing exaggeratedly into my room.

"Yes, I'm awake." I force my eyes open painfully to look at her. She is so small, and I can't imagine how I could have left her for so long. Hoping that the sickness will pass, I reach out and pull her into my arms. Her small limbs come tightly around me and I hold her for a long time. Burying my face in her hair, I breathe her into me. A few soft tears seep down my cheeks unnoticeable.

"I love you so much," I whisper into her ear. I could have held on to her forever, feeling her chest rise and fall against mine.

"I love you too, Kitty," Allie replies, and then pulls her face away from my shoulder to look at me. "Are you ready? Today is the day."

Today? What was today? Allie anxiously searches my face until the realization washes over me.

"Today is grocery day," I state quietly. I have not noticed how quickly the days have passed.

A Veil of Shattered Dreams

And now our day of reckoning is upon us. A nervous excitement begins to build inside of my chest. Allie nods and squirms around in my arms, trying to wriggle out of my grasp. Letting her go, I rise to my feet and head around to the other side of my bed. Using the weak light of Uncle's flashlight that I had kept from the Warehouse to see, I pull out the already packed knapsacks and the sleeping bags from under my bed.

I don't know what will happen after today. But right now, right in this moment, I want to hold on to the calm and embrace the last few hours of this serenity. From this day on I know that whatever happens, I won't be coming back here. There is bitter sweetness in my thoughts. Somehow I have grown fond of this room, the refuge it has provided me against Uncle's tyranny. It has served as the place where Allie and I can be together in a brief peace. And it has been a portal to another world.

"As soon as I check to make sure everything is here, Allie, we're going to take this stuff downstairs and hide it in the Warehouse stairwell. After you take Gramma's purse, we'll grab our stuff before we head out."

"Okay. But don't you think Uncle will check there before he leaves for work?" Allie asks nervously.

"No, he never checks the Warehouse before he leaves for work. Our stuff will be fine there. We can't risk coming back upstairs while they're up here and it would be dumb to put it in the coat closet."

"Okay," Allie agrees and comes over and picks up one of the knapsacks and slings it over her shoulder, carrying the other knapsack in her arms. Hoisting both sleeping bags into my arms, we creep silently out of my room and into the hall. Allie steps out first, treading as softly as she can on the carpet. Night still hangs over the house and I can only hope that it masks our endeavor. Allie is much smaller than me and makes it to the top of the steps without causing any disturbances. She looks back at me, not questioning what she should do next, but waiting for me, making sure that I make it down the hallway.

I take a step and I feel the bulkiness of the sleeping bags work against me. Over the top of the sleeping bag, I nod at Allie. She waits only a few seconds more as I manage to make it to the top of the stairs. One of the sleeping bags is sliding against my slippery palms. Taking a too zealous chance to help me, Allie reaches out to grasp one of the sleeping bags but knocks it from my hands. I watch in horror as the roll tumbles down the stairs, thumping audibly on each step. Allie starts to go down to it, but I lean out and take hold of her shoulder, feeling her small body tremble. Shaking my head, I take my hand off her shoulder and put my finger to my lips in a hushing gesture. If we are caught now, we're done. Straining my ears, the house is still blessedly silent.

Deciding that it is safe, I mouth *"Okay"* to Allie and she quickly tiptoes down to the bottom of the steps and retrieves the sleeping bag. I follow her down and head past her into the hall and carefully find the door to the Warehouse. It creaks loudly as I open it. Shoving the sleeping bag onto the top step, I feel Allie at my back. I turn around and take her stuff from her and place it inside the stairwell. Closing the door with a soft 'click', I make my way back to the staircase, Allie right behind me.

"Okay, we're all set," I whisper and we ascend the staircase swiftly and sneak down the hall towards my room. Just as I make it to my bedroom door, I realize that there is a lack of muted Allie footsteps behind me. Suddenly, my heart stops and I hear thickening thumping footsteps that are too heavy to be Allie's. I glance over at Allie from my bedroom door. She is frozen on the second to last top step. But before I can go back and get her, the large dark silhouette of Uncle treads into the hall. With his back turned to my room, his path is focused solely on Allie. I want to run past him and pull her out of harm's way, but it is out of my control. If I'm exposed, then there is nothing that can stop him from figuring out our plan. Trusting Allie, I peek on from afar.

"Aaand just where do you think you're going this early?" Uncle's voice speaks harshly, but the words are slurred with sleep. *Allie,* I say to her in my mind. *Be strong, be brave.* I see her staring at him in the morning light that is beginning to rise and bathe the house. There is no fear in her face as the bluish glow illuminates her. Today she is determined. In that moment, the defiance in her eyes was the same as I had witnessed in my very own. Every day she seems older than the last.

"I was getting a drink of water," she responds naturally as if Uncle has asked a very stupid question.

A Veil of Shattered Dreams

"Don't lie to me, I heard noises."

"I tripped up the steps. It's dark," Allie reasons. Stupefied by her continued poise and plausible answers, he continues to stare at her menacingly. My insides are cheering and I have never been more proud of her in my life. Seeing Uncle turn around, I quickly duck into my room as to not be seen. I hear his footsteps thudding towards my room. I make a dash for my bed and manage to relax just in time as he appears in the doorframe and flips on the light.

"Get up! Put your damn clothes on. Get your sister ready. Your grandmother will be here for breakfast and I will not have the members of this house lying around like fat whores sucking me dry. Have some pride for fuck's sake," he snarls.

He storms out of sight and in my head, I am already counting the hours until all of this is finally over. I climb out of bed and head over to the bathroom. The morning is upon us now, shining brightly and lighting the whole second floor. I shower fast and pull on the best clothes that I have. Taking a brush through my tangled wet hair, I pad over to check on Allie. She is wearing a light pink dress that I had forgotten she had, with matching sandals.

"I've got to look my best when Daddy sees me," she says and I smile.

"You look beautiful," I reply and braid her long brown hair into a simple plait down her back. Our tender second ends with the sound of the front door banging open and a scuffle of voices and footsteps from the hall.

"And where's breakfast? I thought we were having breakfast? After everything I do for you, you always insist on wasting my time! Just move, get out of my way!" Gramma's screech echoes through the house.

"I've been trying to get them up Mom, but they're just so useless, like you say," Uncle whines, something I've never heard him do before.

"Oh just shut up. I blame you. You call yourself the head of the household? I'm ashamed. Both of my children are a discredit to me." Their voices are growing nearer as they climb the stairs and, to avoid an even bigger confrontation, Allie and I hurry to meet them at the top of the stairs.

"We're right here Gramma," I say.

"Well, then where in the hell is that worthless piece of flesh you call your wife?" Gramma demands.

A Veil of Shattered Dreams

"She's really ill. She won't get up," Uncle answers meekly.

Then Uncle pushes in front of her, pointing his finger at us, and orders, "Go put breakfast on." Gramma pushes his hand out of the way in irritation and we dodge past them and start down the steps.

"What do you mean she won't get up?" Gramma asks angrily. "Well, we'll just have to see about that." She and Uncle start down the hall toward his bedroom.

Downstairs, Allie and I go into the kitchen. If it had been any other day, we would have procrastinated, or we would have found some way to sabotage his requests. But today is different. We're leaving today and I'm determined to make this the best breakfast that we've ever had here. Opening the fridge, I pull out a carton of eggs, a tub of butter, and a jug of orange juice. Placing the orange juice on the table, I notice Allie, stack of plates in hand, beginning to set the table.

One perfect day. That is all we need, one day that our plans work out without incident. I have never felt better. Placing the frying pan on the stove, I concentrate on making scrambled eggs. Just as I spread the butter into the pan, the ghost woman appears in the kitchen. She looks horrible. Her hair is whipped in every direction and red eyes look out from beneath puffy eyelids. She takes a step toward me, but her legs wobble with her own weight. The smell of cooking food wafts through the air and the ghost woman's pallid face is glistening with a thin sheen of sweat.

"Auntie," Allie cries gently, "are you alright?"

She tries to step again and looks like she might be sick all over the kitchen floor. Gramma appears behind the ghost woman and grabs her by the arm. Jerking her forcefully, Gramma sits the ghost woman in one of the empty chairs at the table. I continue to gawk at the ghost woman. I have never seen her like this before. Allie hurries over and takes a seat next to the ghost woman, staring at her concernedly.

"What are you staring at, Katerina?" Gramma snaps angrily.

"Nothing," I reply and quickly turn back to my eggs.

"Go ahead! Look at this piece of filth! Let her serve as a lesson to the both of you! Keep doing what you're doing and you'll end up the same!" Gramma shrieks. Just as Gramma gathers enough wind to strike again, Uncle enters the room and sits down at the head of the table.

"Get up you disgraceful worm! I don't think I could bear you at the head of the table," Gramma rants in disgust.

Uncle is struck dumb and when he freezes on the spot, Gramma raises her voice hysterically. "Look at your wife! My son! My only son! You are a disappointment to me! Have you ever thought how this affects me? Get up!" I never thought I would see humiliation on Uncle's face, but she cut him to the quick. Anger and pain are boiling over his features as he moves over into a side chair.

"Katerina!" she snaps at me. "Where is the damn breakfast?"

"It's right here, Gramma," I say meekly and spoon the eggs into a bowl. Setting the bowl on the table, I quickly sit down across from Allie. The ghost woman groans and the entire table goes quiet. Gramma watches Uncle like a hawk.

"Tell me," Gramma begins dramatically after a long heavy pause, "tell me where I have gone wrong? How am I to bear it?" I scoop a spoonful of eggs onto Allie's and mines plates. The ghost woman gags again and it seems to be more than Uncle can bear. He slams his silverware down on the table and, glaring at Gramma, stands up and storms out of the room.

"Coward! Just like your father! Go on! Leave, run away to your pathetic job." She laughs derisively. From the table, we can hear the front door open and slam forcefully. I have never wanted to be farther from that table in my whole life. Gramma stands up and grabs ahold of the ghost woman by both arms. I have never seen the ghost woman look so depleted in the entire time that we have been here. Her eyes are almost glassy and she gazes around as if she's floating. Dragging her away from the table, Gramma pushes the ghost woman into the hall and out of sight.

"Now, Allie," I say and jump up to make sure the ghost woman and Gramma are out of sight. Allie's eyes are wide and still pointed in the direction of the ghost woman.

"Allie, come on. We don't have much time." Allie looks up at me with shining tears in her eyes.

"We can't just leave her, Kitty." She looks fearful, not for herself, not for me, but for the ghost woman. I am absolutely speechless. Only Allie.

"We have to, we've got to follow the plan. You've got to stay with me. And I can't stay here any longer."

"I can't leave her like this! See what they've done to her, Kitty? What if it were me?"

Damn it. I rub my hand over my face agitatedly. I swear sometimes she is more of an adult than I am. But time is running out and it's now or never. Things with Allie are never simple. I can practically feel the freedom, taste the cool breeze on my lips. All of it is nothing, means nothing without her.

"I'm not going without her," Allie retorts defiantly.

"I'm not leaving you," I say. I can't even believe that we are having this conversation. "Don't you want to see Daddy? Don't you want to go to the creek with me? Don't you want to be happy with me, get away from this place?" Allie nods.

"Yes."

"Okay, then. Look Allie, we've got to go now. Look, maybe once we find Dad and get settled, we can come back for her. Or we can at least call someone. We won't ever be able to get her any help unless we get out of here."

Allie nods, but still looks doubtful.

"I'm going to go and put our stuff in the car. Grab Gramma's purse and wait for me at the door, and then I'll lock them in." Rising up from the table, I walk out into the hallway and listen as Gramma continues to belittle the ghost woman in the upstairs bathroom.

Moving rapidly down the hall to the Warehouse door, I reach inside and grab the knapsacks and carry them and the sleeping bags into the hall. Allie meets me at the front door, holding Gramma's purse in her little arms. I dig around in the purse until I find the keys.

"Go see Gramma and Auntie, make sure they still don't know anything. I'll be right back."

"Okay." Allie scurries away back down the hall and up the stairs.

I slide the door open and step outside. It is a beautiful summer day. The sun is blazing and there is a gentle wind that tugs playfully at my hair. My heart feels immediately lighter and the realization of what I am doing finally sets in. I never want to go back into that house. The lightness threatens to make my head swoon.

Gramma's small station wagon is parked right in the driveway, and I hurry over to it, my burden feeling unbelievably light. At the car, I sit our belongings on the ground and unlock the door. I pile all of the stuff into the back seat and then quietly shut the door. Looking up, I gaze into the distance, at the long winding road that is our future. But something mars the distance, a little black blot, which is zooming rapidly into view. From this far out, I can barely make out the black truck. Uncle's truck. My heart that has felt so light now sinks into my chest like a dead weight. Frantically, I turn and run back to the house. Swinging the door open wildly, not caring any longer about secrecy, I scour the hall and the first floor for Allie.

"Allie!" I yell, "Allie where are you?" I glance back at the wide open door, watching the black truck grow larger as it draws nearer and nearer.

"ALLIE!" I am shouting now and without concern for anyone else who can hear me. Suddenly she appears at the top of the steps. But then another figure fills in the space behind her. Gramma. Gramma is clutching her purse in one hand and Allie in the other.

"I caught you didn't I! Damn little thief!?" Gramma snarls.

"Come on Allie!" I shout. My head is pounding, almost threatening. We have to leave now. Ducking and pulling suddenly out of Gramma's grasp, Allie runs down the steps. Gramma lets out a shout of rage and starts down the stairs in pursuit. I hold out my hand and Allie grabs it. Pulling her through the open door, I slam it shut. "Get in the car! It's unlocked! GO!" I scream and let go of Allie's hand.

Taking the keys from my pocket, I manage to lock the front door just in time. Hearing Gramma's angry shrieks and harsh pounding on the door motivates us to make a beeline for the car. Allie and I jump in, completely out of breath. I put the key into the ignition and hear the old station wagon engine sputter, but not start. *Really? Could this actually be happening?* Allie shoots me a panicky look as I keep trying to start the car with no avail.

Suddenly Allie screams and I look fearfully over my shoulder to see why. Uncle's truck is no longer far down the road; it's nearly here. In desperation, I try to start the car again and it finally comes to life with a roar. Relief mixed with a lingering fear has my hands shaking on the steering wheel. I shift the car into reverse and it

A Veil of Shattered Dreams

lurches wildly backwards, our supplies tumbling precariously to the floorboard.

"Kitty!" Allie cries fearfully, but I manage to maneuver the car out to the end of the drive. The black truck encroaches and is nearly upon us. I can almost see Uncle when the truck suddenly whizzes past the driveway. The driver doesn't even slow. Doesn't even look.

"It's not him!" I cry out in disbelief. "Allie, it's not him!" A crushing wave of relief and happiness floods through me. I press lightly on the gas pedal and the car continues onto the roadway. Shifting the car into drive, I take a deep breath and start down the road.

"We made it, Allie! We made it!" The joy is too much. It threatens to consume me. I look over at Allie and see she is beaming brightly. She is the most lovely and precious thing I have ever seen. I did it! I did it for her.

The dark road flies underneath our tires and I gaze back into my rearview mirror. Uncle's house is rapidly receding into the distance. I look out the chipped and bug-splattered windshield onto the long black road in front of us, the bright morning sunshine beckoning us away from our bleak existence. Allie looks over at me, tears washing down her cheeks.

"Why are you crying?" I ask worriedly.

"Because I'm happy," Allie replies with a cheesy grin. "I love you, Kitty."

"I love you too, Allie. I told you I would get us out of there."

We are free. And for once it seems that one of my promises might actually come true. The road bends and my speed picks up as the car adds distance between us and our old lives. Memories of our old lives are already fading as Uncle's house disappears from view as I navigate the bend.

"Kitty!" Allie exclaims, pointing at the road in front of us. The road straightens and the path that the car is taking is quickly sending us toward a guardrail. I try to yank the wheel back, but I can't. Allie screams. And the scream is so deafening that it drowns out everything else. All conscious thought gone.

It was like in one moment, we were infinite, that I would keep driving and driving until the road ran out. And it was gone in the next, in a flurry of cruel metal and blinding light. Allie's screams fill my ears. In half a heartbeat, we impact, my head smashing into the steering wheel.

Woozily, I sit up and look over at Allie's crumpled form. And I watch helplessly as the light leaves her eyes.

And then I shatter.

I'm ripped painfully from my body until the only thing that remains is the deeply scarred truth. It's like someone has taken a scalpel to my brain and scraped the illusion away. The illusion that has become a tantalizing torment to me when I refused to see the truth.

Allie is gone.

I am the pulse point and the pulse point is me.

In my heart, there is an inconsolable grief for Allie and for the half-life that I imprisoned her in for so long. I just could never let her go. The veil rips away and everything sears through my mind, filling it up with an overwhelming chaos too great to bear. The scorching pain sears like liquid flames melding two shattered halves into a whole.

I remember. I remember everything.

Memories

Allie is running toward me, her soft chestnut hair flapping wildly behind her. Strands of hair strains against the movement and are released off her body.

"Allie!" I cry and beckon her closer. As her tiny feet hit the ground, first one then the other, her skin cracks, leaving pitted lines in her sweet features. As she runs, the cracks deepen into her skin.

"Kitty!" Allie shouts fearfully. She is almost to me and I take off sprinting so I can meet her. As she gets closer, bits of her face and hands break away, flaking off and disintegrating rapidly into nothingness.

I extend my arms out, ready to embrace her. Her eyes are shining and I see the fear leaving them as our fingers go to touch. But with a sickening crunch, Allie splinters and pieces of her shatter into a pile in front of me.

"ALLIE! ALLIE!" I scream over and over as I crumple to the ground, gathering the debris. Sifting through the glittering pieces, I fill my hands with the razor-like slivers. The jagged shards slice into my skin and hot droplets of blood ooze out, trickling down my wrists and arms. Sobbing, I gather as many pieces as I can and hug them close to me, not caring as they pierce my skin and slit my chest and arms. Fresh blood seeps over the debris and I lie down with it covering me.

"Allie," I whimper painfully. My sister. My child. She was everything that anyone could be to me. But even all the love that I had to offer her in the world, every drop that I could squeeze from my withering veins, was not enough. And now she is severed and even the memories and all the thoughts are only an incapacitating ache that won't let me go. A piece that I have been clutching in my hand has etched itself deep into the skin. Prying the drenched fragment from the broken flesh, I bring it to my face and prick each of my cheeks so that the crimson flows like tears.

A grief-stricken moan escapes my lips and I can taste the warm metallic tang of red on my tongue. I grip the fragment tightly, wanting to mold it back into my hand, but it slips and smashes as it falls from my grasp. I lay with my hair sprawled out, matted in congealing blood, my body cut raw, prickling with hot pain beyond the physical realms of reality. Pain that incinerates, cauterizing nerves into numbness. Grief gives way to guilt. I look up, but am swallowed by a bottomless black ocean. I cannot think, breathe, or move.

"ALLIE'S DEAD!" I howl and the words are agony as they are ripped from my lips. "Gone! My baby sister, my baby girl!" As I open my eyes, they finally reveal the truth and I let the crippling sobs wrack my body. "My baby sister, my baby..." Tremors hit me and I shake uncontrollably as the sorrow is unleashed in an irrepressible torrent of screams and sadness.

"Katerina! Katerina can you hear me? It's happening! Katerina!" a frenzied voice is barely audible over my internal distress. I can almost make her out behind the blurred veil of tears streaming down my face. She is standing across from me holding something small and round in her hands. Sticking her head out the door, the woman shouts frantically into the hall, "Someone get Sanjay now! It's an emergency! Tell him that it's happening!"

The woman rushes over to me and tries to grasp one of my hands in hers. But her fingers feel like knives tearing at my flesh. I pull away violently, trying to get away. But something is solidifying around me and my hands become trapped inside thick white fabric. The more I try to wrestle and tear at it, the more tangled I become. The fabric becomes twisted around my body and my neck.

"Katerina! Stop! You're going to injure yourself!" I suck in deeply to try and catch my breath but the cloth suctions itself to my mouth and the air catches in my lungs. Trying to rip the cloth from my face, it billows around me and I sink lower, entombed in it. The space is hot and damp and the white is now mixed with pools of black beading in and out of my sight.

"SANJAY! Hurry!" The woman yells and the scuffle of footsteps and voices answer her. Suddenly the woman and the noises seem far away and I'm drifting quietly, the sounds almost silent. Almost peaceful.

Then the white is yanked off of my head and the cool air rushes in, filling my lungs with its soothing flow.

"Katerina, are you awake?" A man's voice cuts in firmly. I look up to see him standing over me. His eyes, framed by black-rimmed glasses, are full of concern.

"What happened Katerina, tell me what happened?" I hear his voice, but I can't comprehend any of the words. The excruciating agony of debilitating grief explodes through me again as the flashes of memory batter through my ravaged brain.

Waking up was like emerging from the end of a long dark tunnel into the light. In my body there was an awkward stiffness, but nothing was hurting. But then I recognized the artificial peace of painkillers, the white noise of an IV pump, and the confusion of not knowing where you were before you arrived there. The flutter of opening eyes changed everything and plunged me into awareness.

"Kitty Kat! She's awake! Can you hear me Kitty? It's Daddy! Someone call a nurse, Katerina's waking up!"

"Daddy?" I mumbled blearily.

"It's okay Kitty, I'm here."

"Daddy, what happened to me?" I asked, feeling the tiny wisps of fear and anxiety shoot through my body. I looked at him and the pain contorted on his face. He began to tremble as he spoke.

"Baby, there was an accident. In the car, remember? You were coming home from the movies, remember?" A flicker of a dark memory surrounded my conscious.

"Allie?" I questioned, paralyzing dread growing inside my heart. Daddy's face succumbed to a mass of silent tears and deep heaving breaths. He shook his head, raising his hands to cover his face.

"She didn't make it."

"What?" I cried out in disbelief.

"Allie's gone."

I clutch my hands to my face, weeping wildly through my fingers. The ponytailed man grasps ahold of my arms, trying to steady me.

"Katerina, listen to me. Everything is going to be all right. You just need to calm down. Take some deep breaths." I gasp and swallow a mouthful of air. It sends me into a fit of coughing that has me spitting up and choking on my own tears.

It was raining the day Allie was buried. The grass had been churned into a muddy brown that left imprints of those who had come to pay their respects. The grief stripped me to the bone as they lowered her tiny casket into the ground. It was too small. I had never seen a casket so small. I imagined her little body lying under the earth century after century, when all she had ever wanted was to live in the sun. Which is where I hoped she was now. But I was too selfish and I wanted her here with me. I wanted her to be alive more than I wanted to be. My sorrow was a mountain and the weight of it brought me to my knees, deep down in the sodden earth. The cold rain dumped buckets and buckets down, gnawing at my sensitive flesh so that the chill embedded into my body and my soul.

"Come on Katerina, it's time to go." My mother's hollow voice penetrated my thoughts. She gripped my shoulders with her bony hands, encouraging me to get up from the ground.

Wailing, I screamed, "I can't leave her! I can't leave her here! She needs me! She needs me!"

The screams faded into desolate but silent anguish and I dug my hands down into the squelching earth, determined to stay rooted right there. I never wanted to leave her side.

My heart is racing now and sweat is beading against my forehead. The beads slide down onto my trembling lips, mixing with salty tears. My chest is thumping harshly as the burn of my loss rips through me. I try to breathe, but my throat is narrowing. I sputter and gasp.

"Bring me a light sedative. She's having a panic attack. We've got to calm her down." The man orders, his hands gripping my arms firmly. I struggle against his hold, but it is strong and unyielding.

"I've got you Katerina, I've got you." The man says gently, but my hysteria is unending.

Allie had just seen a movie in the theater for the first time. She was bubbling with excitement as the room darkened and the first preview appeared. I had never seen her happier. Her happiness fed my own. It was all I needed in the world. She was the most wonderful thing in my life, from her soft crooked smiles to her quick-witted responses, too old for a person so young. As our mother deteriorated in both beauty and character, surrendering to the darkness inside of her, Allie had blossomed. She was the embodiment of health and goodness. She was mine and I was hers.

After the movie, we settled into the car and Allie quickly fastened herself into her car seat. She was so smart and sometimes more responsible than me. And as the road flowed smoothly under us, leading us home, I thought there couldn't be anything better than this in the entire world. But the car had other plans, slamming us into a guardrail and flipping us over and over down a steep bank.

"All my fault," I whimper, "I killed her."

"What's your fault, Katerina?" The man asks. Another person enters the room hurriedly and hands him a small white tube. He uncaps the end of the tube to reveal a thin, barely there needle. "Louise, come over here and swab her. Quickly." The woman who I had recoiled from hurries over. She swipes a small wet pad gingerly on my arm that the man is holding. Swiftly, the man brings the syringe down and injects something deftly under my skin.

"It'll help with the pain. Whatever you're dealing with."

"How much?"

"For you Pretty Thing, $20." I reached into my hoodie pocket and pulled out a crumpled $20 dollar bill.

A Veil of Shattered Dreams

"I like the way you do business." He handed me a small plastic baggie with a chunk in it about the size of two breath mints side by side. Tucking the baggie inside of my shirt, I turned around and ran.

I said I was tutoring students that day. Dad believed me. He was worried about me, but glad that I had taken up such a positive hobby. I laughed scathingly at my own deception; I couldn't even remember the person I had once been. I only knew that my loss was too much to endure. That everything, even the simple notion of being alive, reminded me of her, of the guilt that had rooted itself so deep in my heart. And I know she would have detested the person I had become. But she caused this suffering. If she had only stayed alive for me, her memory wouldn't have taunted the masochist inside.

The memory is too much to bear. It is still too fresh, too new. It knocks me back into life.

"Katerina!" I hear a shout above the dwindling chaos in the room.

"Get him out of here," the man says quietly, "this is crucial to her recovery. He doesn't need to be here right now."

"Is she awake? Really awake? Katerina!" the shout comes again and I recognize the familiar voice that has been with me in my thoughts and in my dreams the whole time.

"Leon," I gasp. It hadn't been a dream. Leon was there. He was there for me. And now he is here and I want to fight through my crushing grief to tell him how sorry and grateful I am.

"Calm down, Katerina. Everything is going to be just fine. You need to rest your mind. Concentrate and tell me what happened," the man urges.

Liquid tranquility is spilling inside of me; there is an unnatural peace that combats the madness and pulls me out of the pain. I take a deep breath and let it fill my lungs. My chest expands and I feel a weight evaporate off of my body.

"Leon?" I ask anxiously, looking around for him, struggling to throw off my restrictive sheets.

"I'm here!" Leon's voice assures.

"Leon's here. It's okay, tell us what happened," the man repeats.

"I remember," I say, fresh tears flowing down my face. "Allie. The car…" but I falter and I'm suddenly feeling drowsy. "I don't want to go back

A Veil of Shattered Dreams

to sleep," I protest groggily. But I can't stop the overwhelming feeling of lethargy that is coming over me.

There is something infinitely comforting about nothingness, about floating, about slipping into the void. Soundless, wordless, colorless, but painless too, and oh so gentle. I'm everywhere and nowhere and it's a kind of empty little bliss. But the world won't let me go. It pulls me back, back beyond the veil of shattered dreams to pick up the fragments and wear them like badges of courage. Not to relive, but to rebuild. To begin again.

When I awake, everything is as if I'm seeing it for the first time. I glance over at the window with bright sunlight streaming through. The light dances and reflects off the floor, bouncing into my eyes. A smile spreads across my lips. I've been through the grief, the fire, the all-consuming void, and I've returned. I'm ready now.

Rising from my bed, I plant my feet firmly onto the floor, grounded. For the first time in a long time, I feel like I won't be pulled away and that the invisible hand is no longer near. Shuffling quickly into my slippers and wrapping my robe around me, I make my way over to the window ledge next to the door. The photo is still there. I pick up the frame and gaze into it. Allie and me. Allie and me like we always were, like we always will be.

"You didn't have your scar then." I remember Leon saying. It seems like years have passed since I last heard his voice. I reach up instinctively to touch my forehead to feel the soft indentation of a long thin scar. The accident. And now I know why I would never let myself remember. The guilt had been too much, too unbearable to store into memory. But now it has marked me, branding me so that I will never forget. After living so long without it, after shutting it out, I never want to forget again. A single tear escapes from my eye and slides down my cheek, splattering onto the glass frame. Brushing the tear from the glass, I place the frame back on the ledge.

The door to my room opens and startles me. And my surprise is mirrored in the faces of the three people who walk in.

"Katerina! You're up! That's fantastic!" A kind and enthusiastic male voice exclaims and now I can put a name to the kind doctor with the glasses who was there when I shattered. He comes over and begins to examine me quickly, feeling my pulse and checking for any signs of lingering hysteria.

"Yes, yes I am, and I'm ready, Sanjay," I reply calmly and clearly.

"Are you sure? You've been through a lot today already," a different male voice cuts in. A voice I would have recognized anywhere. He steps from behind Sanjay and smiles his infectious smile.

"Leon," I say. And just saying his name and realizing all that he has meant and all that he has done for me, brings the brightest smile to my face. I try to convey all my gratitude, all my relief and warmness through my wide stare.

"Are you feeling okay? Do you want to sit down? Do you want to eat something, Katerina dear?" Another familiar voice permeates the air.

"I'm fine, Mrs. Babbitt. Really. Thanks. But," I say, looking seriously at Sanjay, "I think it's time. I need to let it go now."

Nodding understandingly, Sanjay replies, "Of course. We have a session in twenty minutes that I was preparing for. Are you ready to join us?" I look at Sanjay and then glance over at Leon. His blue eyes are twinkling encouragingly.

"Yes, I am. Do you mind if Leon walks me down?" I ask and Leon's eyes glow brighter.

"Not at all. We'll see you down there in about ten minutes." I nod and Sanjay's face looks how I feel, a bundle of joy and relief.

"See you then," I agree brightly.

"I'll be at the nurse's station if you need anything," Mrs. Babbitt reassures and steps out of the room, leaving the door open.

As she leaves, I turn to Leon and try to find the words that I want to say to him. But nothing seems to be enough.

"Leon," I begin, "I'm so sorry. I must have been a lot of trouble for you."

Leon interrupts incredulous, "Katerina, it's nothing. Absolutely nothing compared to what you went through."

"But I was gone for so long, I was so scared."

"I still would have been here. I'm not going anywhere. I'm here for you," he asserts.

Tears begin to well in my eyes, not of sadness, but of gratitude, for having someone like him be a part of my life. As they spill over my cheeks, I can't stop myself from pulling him in for an embrace.

"Thank you," I whisper, "thank you for being my rock."

"I'm here if you need me," he replies, pulling out of the hug and stepping back, locking those big blue eyes with mine.

Looking away self-consciously, Leon clears his throat and states, "We better get going or Sanjay may think that you changed your mind."

"No, I'm ready for this."

"Okay then." he leads me out of the room and we walk down the hallway. As we turn a corner, a tall figure of a man heads directly for us. As he grows nearer, a smile lights up my face.

"Howdy there Leon! I see you brought me a little present! Ain't you a sight for sore eyes! I'm here to finish escorting Kat darlin' down to the session." He extends one of his large tattoo covered arms out to me.

"Randy!" I exclaim and the happiness that I feel at recognizing him explodes inside of me. Leaving Leon's side, I clasp a hold of Randy's arm. I barely notice Leon leaving until he is almost halfway back down the hall.

"Leon!" I call back to him. "I'll see you later?" He turns around and I wave at him.

"See you later," he replies back with a wave before turning around and continuing on his way.

"I'm so glad you're back," Randy says sincerely as we continue on to the session room. "I knew you'd come around. You're a fighter, Katerina."

"I don't know if I can do this," I admit, feeling the nervousness and grief begin to rise in my gut.

"Yes, you can, Kat. I see so much of myself in you. You've been through hell and back and collected a couple battle scars, but they're nothing to be ashamed of. I've been there. I've been there on both sides of the needle too. I've been to the bottom, not knowing whether I'd ever see the light of day again. But my morning came, and today, well Kat baby, today is your day."

We arrive at the room and Randy pushes the door open for me. "Come sit next to me," he says and gestures over to two empty chairs sitting side by side. As we walk in, all eyes are on us. The twins are there, exactly the same as I had always remembered them and then, as I turn my head around, my eyes fall upon the most familiar face in the entire room.

The ghost woman.

A Veil of Shattered Dreams

She is here, and she is part of every reality that I have ever known. If it wasn't for her, I would have never been able to find this peace in my heart. She played an instrumental role in my recovery, had fueled my fire. She had been there through everything, to see me in my darkest hour as my own conscience. Without her, I would have never been able to forgive myself.

Sitting down, my gaze never leaves hers. She isn't fading anymore. Something has changed her, just as she has changed me.

"Okay everyone," Sanjay begins, "I would like to take this moment to once again welcome Katerina back into our circle. And I think that Katerina actually has something that she wants to share with us today. Katerina?" I nod, but as soon as his words finish and the spotlight turns to me, I feel the bundle of nerves and emotions building inside of me.

I don't know if I can make the words come to my lips. I close my eyes and the image of Allie floods my mind, my senses, my whole being, as if she is still here, still a part of me. A tear droplet falls. I miss her so much, so terribly that I want collapse into my grief.

Randy's hand massages my shoulder soothingly. "You can do it, Kat. Tell us all about it," he encourages and keeps me from losing my composure completely.

I take in a long ragged deep breath. I can be strong. I can be strong for Allie. I can be strong for myself. The mountains that I have built around me are beginning to crumble, and the avalanche of everything that I have been holding back washes away my reserves like a riptide.

"I loved my sister Allie more than anything in the world," I begin quietly, thinking back fondly on her crooked little smile. "She just had this way about her that was uplifting. Like she was pure spirit trapped in the body of a little girl. I would have given anything for her. She was the most wonderful little child on the whole planet. I wanted to give her everything that our mother couldn't. Our mother, though we are alike in so many ways, let her emptiness and her darkness consume her," I explain, remembering how I watched my mother stare blankly at the walls of our home. Watched in my reconstructed memory as my father begged her, *"Please baby, please feel something."*

"The day Allie was born," I continue, "I was eleven years old and even then I felt the need to fill our mother's absence, to fill the hole she left with her callousness and her detached emotions.

"So, I raised Allie. I took care of her when our father was out working, or looking for work. I taught her how to say the alphabet and how to read. She was just so full of life." I felt the guilt rise up, bitter and threatening to pull me back under.

"And then I took it from her. I took that life from her and I'll never be able to give it back. It's all my fault she died in the car wreck!" The words squeeze themselves out of my mouth. I am ashamed. I feel responsible and vulnerable and I want to dive back into my own madness and forget everything that is happening.

"Katerina, it wasn't your fault. There was nothing you could do. You didn't do anything wrong. According to the accident report, the steering on the car locked up. It malfunctioned. See, it wasn't your fault." Sanjay interrupts.

Malfunctioned? There was a thought that had never occurred to me before, a thought with a small glimmer of hope attached to it. I hold on to that glimmer of hope and cradle its warmth close to me. Maybe I was worthy of redemption after all.

"It wasn't my fault?" I repeat hesitantly, hearing the words fall from my mouth with my own ears.

"No, Kat. You wouldn't believe how often that happens. Hell, I remember when my front tire blew out on me one time and I couldn't get control of the car no matter how hard I turned that damn wheel. Shit like that happens. There was probably nothing that you, or anybody else, could have done," Randy interjects.

Can my shattered heart beat again? I want to believe it can. But still, how can I possibly be happy when Allie is dead?

"Why couldn't it have been me?" I cry, the torrents of emotions pouring out of me through my tears. "I spent so many nights wishing that I was the one dead. Hoping that I didn't have to go on living without her." I sob and recall the many heroin nights, when even the strongest high couldn't keep all the misery at bay. "Even when I wanted to forget, I woke up feeling guilty about forgetting. It was crushing me and all I wanted was to make it go away. I wanted to make myself go away. I hated myself in every single way," I

A Veil of Shattered Dreams

admit shamefully and the veracity of the truth sets all of my tears free.

I let myself weep for my loss, for everything that I have done. I grieve for Allie's life that was prematurely cut short in a matter of mere seconds. I grieve for myself for not having the courage to remember my sister the way that I should have, and then condemning us to live in a nightmare for so long. I was selfish. It was the only way that I could keep her with me. I cry for a long time and no one stops me, not Sanjay, not Randy, who only squeezes my shoulder, letting me know that he's there.

Just when I think that I cannot cry anymore, I gaze at Sanjay through my tears for answers. The pain is subsiding, still there, but manageable. It will always be there. Through the last of my tears, I cry out with the residue of agony in my soul.

"Why couldn't Allie have lived?" I shriek. "I wanted her to live!" I feel Randy's hand soothe me again, feel all the emotions dump out of me and then resettle.

"She does live," Sanjay says, "Allie will always live. Allie lives in you, Katerina. You keep her alive in your spirit, in your memories." Behind my closed eyes, I see Allie again. She is smiling at me from out of a glass frame. Not out of a picture, but out of my own reflection. I watch as she rises up out of me and suspends her grinning face in the air. Clinging to my hand, she waits, looking down at me. I have never seen her so content, so peaceful. She tugs at me to go with her, but I smile with a final tear glistening down my cheek. And then I do the unthinkable.

    I let her go.

Epilogue

(2 Months Later)

"You've made quite a recovery, Katerina. I know that I am going to miss you terribly," the doctor said as he came into Katerina's room one last time. "It's hard to believe that you've only been here a few months, but I have complete faith you're on a solid road to full recovery. You've accomplished so much. So much more than some of the patients here could ever dream to achieve."

"Thanks Sanjay. I'm just glad that I get to go home now," Katerina replied, taking one last turn about the room, gathering her duffel bag and suitcase in hand.

"I'm sure that your father has missed you," Sanjay states kindly.

"Actually," came a voice from the outer hallway. "I know he has!"

"DADDY!" Katerina exclaimed, dropping the luggage and running over to her father. "I've missed you so much!" and wrapped her arms around him in a tight bear hug.

"I've missed you more than I can say, Kitty Kat. I just love you so much." He squeezed her tighter and whispered in her ear, "I am never letting you go again."

Katerina smiled. He was here, he was actually here. It seemed like a lifetime since she'd seen her father. Wiping a single tear from his eye, he looked happier than she had seen him in a while. Releasing him, they both turned around to look at Sanjay.

"Katerina, why don't you run down to Louise's office and ask her if she has your discharge papers ready? I want to speak to your father for a few moments," Sanjay suggested gently.

"Okay. I'll be right back," Katerina said and departed the room to run the errand. Once Katerina had gone, Sanjay invited her father to take a seat as he leaned up against the bedframe.

He began to explain in a hushed voice, "Katerina, as you can see, has done extremely well in our inpatient care program. Most other patients require at least six months of intensive treatment, but I am pleased that she has gone far beyond everyone's expectations. There was a time that we grew very concerned. Her delusions were very strong and we were afraid that she might never come back to us. We believe that Katerina's sister played a major role in these delusions."

"Really?" Her father questioned. "And by delusions you mean…?"

"Many people deal with their grief in many different ways. Some find comfort with their loved ones. Some seek counseling. But others like Katerina, find that guilt, such as she felt from the accident, can also be a way of making sense of their sorrow," Sanjay explicated. "The delusional periods," he continued, "that Katerina experienced were her mind's way of dealing with the deep and mixed emotions she was feeling. Katerina receded to some place deep inside of her mind where she tried to keep the image of her sister very real. Often times, she was adamant that she had to get back to Allie."

"She was hallucinating?" the father questioned in confusion.

"No, not really. She had created an alternate universe in her mind where Allie was still alive. In order for this to be real for her, she had to deny reality. Everything she was referring to during her more lucid moments must have happened inside of her head. It was as though she had suppressed all her memories with her grief."

"She seems fine now. What did you do to help her recover?" her father asked concernedly, leaning forward in his chair with interest.

"Well, we used a routine treatment to help her cope with her drug addiction. And then a standard regiment of medication to help calm her mind. After we were confident that the medication was working, we assigned one of our staff members as her mentor. Mentorship establishes trust that builds a foundation for assisting patients in their recovery."

"Our staff member met with Katerina almost every day, working to help coax her out of her darkness. With his help, we were able to gradually reduce her medications," Sanjay explained. "During this time, we kept regular reports and, through her mentor, we monitored her progress. As Katerina was weaned from the medication, she became more lucid and receptive to group therapy. As she began to accept her place back in this reality, she was finally able to come to terms with her sister's death and is now on the road to a full recovery."

A Veil of Shattered Dreams

"Does she need to come back for any kind of checkup at all? Is it possible that she may relapse?" Her father asked with worry in his features.

Before Sanjay could answer, Katerina walked back into the room, holding a stack of paperwork. Eyeing Katerina, Sanjay continued carefully, "Relapse in her current condition is unlikely. However, her outpatient treatment includes continuing group therapy here for the next several months. But Katerina's time as an inpatient with us is over and she is free to go home."

"You hear that kiddo? Time to go home now," Katerina's father said cheerfully.

"Here are the discharge papers from Mrs. Babbitt, Sanjay!" Katerina handed the papers over to Sanjay excitedly.

"Great! Katerina, I am so proud of you," Sanjay praised, clapping a friendly hand on her shoulder. "You should give some thought to participating in our patient mentoring program. We would love to have you work with our staff."

"Patient mentoring?" Katerina asked, intrigued.

"Yes, like Leon. And almost all of our mentors are rehabilitated former patients. We feel that they are the most empathetic to our current patients' situations."

"That sounds like a terrific idea!" Katerina's father interjected.

"Sure Sanjay, I'll definitely consider it," Katerina agreed, picking up her duffel bag off the floor and hoisting it up onto her shoulder.

"Alright, let's get on the road Kitty Kat," he father said, picking up the rest of her belongings and going out into the hallway. Smiling, Katerina gave Sanjay a light hug and then turned around to follow her father.

As they made their way down the long stretch of corridor, Katerina saw the thin outline of a woman resting against the nurse's station window.

"Katerina!" she called out, "I heard you were leaving."

"I am, Charlotte," Katerina replied, walking over to her. Charlotte's eyes were bright and her face colored with life. She was a ghost woman no longer.

"Good luck," Charlotte wished, holding out her hand to Katerina. But Katerina ignored it and went in for a hug instead.

"You will never know how much you have meant to me," Katerina whispered into her ear. "I wish you the very best." Pulling away, Katerina went back to join her father, who was waiting at the front door.

"Kat! You just weren't gonna leave and not say good-bye were ya? Shame on ya!" a familiar voice came from behind her farther back down the hall. She turned around and grinned.

"Randy! I thought you had already left!" Katerina exclaimed, walking back toward him.

"Well, I keep trying to, but Louise keeps giving me more work to do."

"Sanjay asked me to come back and join the mentoring program."

"He did, did he? Well that's awesome! You know I only started doing it a week ago and I think I've found my calling."

"That's really great. Well maybe I will come back then."

"I sure hope so. I'll miss ya!" He leaned down and gave Katerina a small squeezing hug. "But I knew this day would come. You let me know if you need anything, anything at all and big Randy will be there for ya."

"I miss you already," Katerina said, giving him one last little hug and then turned back to her father.

"It seems that you met a lot of good people here," her father observed before pushing the front door open to the outside. It was an achingly beautiful day, with bright sunshine and a clear endless sky. As they walked down the cement sidewalk toward the parking lot, Katerina's father went ahead to the car and she hung back a little bit so she could bask in the afternoon glow.

"KATERINA! KATERINA!" Another voice shouted from behind her and she stopped again, turning around to see a young man sprinting towards her from the entrance. As he approached, out of breath, he said, "Randy told me you just left. I just wanted to come say good-bye."

"Oh, okay, well good-bye. Take care, Leon. Thank you for everything."

"Yeah, good-bye." He stared at her, blue eyes flashing with the words that would not come out of him. "Er, well Randy also said that you were thinking about coming back? As a mentor?"

"Yes, I am. Were you a patient here, then?" Katerina asked inquisitively.

"Umm, yeah I was." Leon replied sheepishly, "But it's a really great program and it inspired me to want to help others," he finished, pausing for her reaction.

"That's really sweet of you. Well maybe if I come back to work here, I'll see you around," Katerina suggested kindheartedly.

"Or, you know, since you're discharged and all, maybe we could go see a movie sometime?" Leon proposed awkwardly. "I mean if you want."

"I would really like that," Katerina answered sincerely.

"Really? Great, I'll see you then."

"See you then," Katerina agreed. She looked over at her father, who was already putting her baggage into his car.

"Oh, and Katerina," Leon interjected, "if you ever need someone to talk to, just call me."

"I will. Thanks Leon. You've been such a good friend to me," she said and smiled. Leon grinned his Leon-grin that Katerina had grown to know so well. Waving, Katerina stepped down off the cement pathway and into the parking lot.

As she headed over toward her father, Katerina thought that she had never felt better. In the back of her mind, a little mass of sadness still remained, but it always would. It was just manageable now.

Allie had always loved beautiful days like this, and as Katerina made her way over to her father's car, she felt Allie everywhere, in everything. She let the feeling surround her and there was no grief. Only acceptance.

About the Author

Rachel Stark has always loved the written word. From the first time she won a writing contest in the second grade, she has continued to write leisurely since. She is an avid reader and loves to write prose as well as poetry. A Veil of Shattered Dreams is her first novel, but probably not her last now that the author bug has bitten.